SOUL OF THE CELLIST

Maddie Evans

Print ISBN: 978-1-942133-43-8
Library of Congress Control Number: 2020952664

Cover art by Crowe Covers
Editing by Michaela DeToma

DEDICATION

Two years ago, I covered a charity 5K for the local paper. A high school senior organized it to promote awareness of early-onset frontotemporal dementia, the illness that was taking her father from her family at far too young an age. I was impressed by her and by her family, touched by their perseverance and their resourcefulness, and by how in the midst of their struggle, they cared about making the way easier for others. Long after the 5K, their experience stuck with me.

Although the Castleton family is in no way based on the Krauss family, I'd like to dedicate the Castleton String Quartet trilogy to the memory of Mark Krauss and to all those who loved and supported him.

CHAPTER ONE

When Hannah asked if her phone was ready, she didn't expect the shop owner to lead her outside the building and shut the door. "I found a problem."

It wasn't full dark yet, even this early in October, but the Maine air had an autumn bite to it. Hannah huddled down in her jacket. "What kind of problem? Is my phone toast?"

"The phone's fine." The repair shop owner, Cashman, had coppery-brown eyes that tended to look right through her. "When you said it was running slow and the power was draining, my first guess was the battery. It turns out the battery's fine, and the phone is loaded with spyware."

Hannah recoiled. "A virus?"

Cashman shook his head. "No, I mean someone deliberately loaded comprehensive monitoring software onto your phone to spy on you. You mentioned the power drain started after you upgraded the OS, so I bet that threw something out of whack. This spy software is insidious. It's constantly monitoring your data, but it also periodically takes photos with the selfie camera and uploads them somewhere. On occasion it turns on the mic to listen to your surroundings. It's tracking your location. Whenever you send a password, it's recording it."

Hannah took an involuntary step backward. Taking photos? Uploading her private conversations?

What had it heard? What had it seen?

Who would even do that? Hannah was the most boring person she knew. If people were spying on glamorous women in New York City—sure. Spy on the beautiful people who attended dinner-dances, not the musicians in black who played for them.

Fighting the urge to run, Hannah closed her eyes and dug her fingers into her palms. Everything she might ever have said, anything she might ever have done—how much of it was in the presence of the phone? Had this random repair guy found records of all of it on the phone and now knew—well, everything?

Cashman folded his arms. "After I realized what I was dealing with, I pulled the battery out of the unit and removed the SIM card, disabled the Wi-Fi and Bluetooth, and locked it in the safe. Leaving the building is probably overkill, but I have no idea how diabolic this thing is. I'm messaging with a few other IT techs right now who think this particular monitoring software can survive a factory reset. My wife told me to call the cops to show them what I've found, but that's your decision, not mine." He glanced at her and started. "You're pale. How about we go back inside and you sit for a minute? And if you have a vindictive ex, I strongly suggest we call the police before you leave."

He held the door for Hannah. As she entered, a bedraggled tabby cat darted in past her ankles.

Spyware? That had to be a mistake. Something that knew all her passwords? It had all her photos? It had tracked her location everywhere since...since when? Who could be so obsessed with Hannah that they needed to know when her string quartet played for a wedding in Bangor?

As she shivered on the couch, Cashman handed her a laptop. "I took screenshots of everything once I realized what we were dealing with, but I didn't want to dig too deep in case the master spy realized what I was doing. Do you know who might have installed it?"

"It's not a vindictive ex. I've never really had a boyfriend." Great, now this guy thought of Hannah not just as a victim but also as a twenty-four-year-old spinster.

Cashman looked surprised. "I'd have bet the house it was an ex. Who else has access to your phone?"

"No one. It's password protected."

Cashman's eyebrows raised. "Is it a secondhand phone? Since the software can theoretically survive a factory reset, maybe the spyware is a holdover from the previous owner."

Oh, no. No—that would be—

Hannah doubled forward with her face in her hands, her fingers pressed to her temples.

Cashman ventured, "Ah. Does it turn out this phone is evidence in a different trial?"

She looked up, blinking hard, mouth trembling. Cashman looked unnerved, and Hannah struggled to keep her voice steady. "How do I make it safe?"

Cashman handed her his laptop. "Assume as of this second that every single online account is compromised. All your social media. Anywhere you've shopped. All your email accounts. For starters, you're going to need to change passwords on everything, but later tonight you'll need to get a new, clean email address, and start using that as your primary. Then go into every single account and de-link it from your current email. And for that, the first thing is to change your current email account passwords."

She logged into Gmail, and Cashman said, "Actually, go into your security," and when she did, he showed her a second IP address also logged in, this one in Hartwell,

Maine. "Lovely." He took a screenshot, then used his phone to search up the IP address. "It's coming from an auto body shop."

Hannah had gone so numb she couldn't feel the laptop under her fingertips. "It's my stepfather. That's where he works. Last Christmas, he gave me this phone."

Cashman wrote a list of the steps Hannah needed to take. While she started doing the impossible, he called the Brighthead Police Department to send a detective, then rummaged in the back shelves until he found a new phone. Well, a new refurbished phone. "It's not quite as good as the one you'll be trading me, but it's clean. I'll attempt to scrub the other phone, but I'd never trust it again."

By the time the detective arrived, Hannah had booted the other user off her account, then immediately changed her password from "1CelloVoice" to "LeaveM3Alone." Then she raced one at a time through all her other accounts. Social media. Shopping. Her bank account.

It was overwhelming, but Cashman's list gave the chaos some order, that way once she started, she'd have the best possible chance of getting through it all before her stepfather realized.

Later tonight, she'd have to do as Cashman said and create another email account, one completely unrelated to this one, and repeat the entire process.

A police officer arrived. Cashman spoke to her first while Hannah continued changing passwords. Her brain had gone mushy. She was using the same password on every site, but it would only stay this way for a few hours. On the next pass she'd create unique unbreakable passwords. Cashman would say that wasn't 'best practices' or something, but it took too much mental power to do anything else.

When she'd gotten through the list, the officer approached. "Cashman showed me the screen shots. The question now is what we do about it."

Cashman said, "Do you have enough to arrest him?"

The officer shook her head. "This qualifies as stalking, but a stalking charge requires a pattern of behavior—at least two incidents. I'll talk to the police in Hartwell, but most likely they'll just go chat with him."

Cashman folded his arms and leaned against one of the workbenches. "Are you sure he isn't dangerous?"

The officer frowned. "The problem is, even if he seems dangerous because he's trying to exert coercive control, that's not something we can prosecute. Cyberstalking, sure. He's violating her privacy. Until he does more than the one incident—and yes, even ten months of monitoring only counts as one incident—we're legally stuck."

Hannah rested her head on the cushions, eyes closed.

The officer said to her, "Has he ever hit you, detained you, verbally abused you?"

Hannah said, "Not like that. He's just difficult."

Cashman said, "You need to talk to a domestic violence hotline. Or a therapist. People like that will get your head all turned around. If you were raised by that man, you've picked up a lot of ideas that probably aren't true, and it takes a long time to break free of them."

The officer sounded concerned. "You had that experience too?"

"Not as overt as hers, but there are a lot of ways to do coercive control. Also," and Cashman sounded momentarily amused, "my wife used to work for a domestic violence agency. She's been blowing up my phone with advice ever since I found the spyware and asked her what to do."

"I'll just ask a few more questions, and then I'll consult our police chief on how to proceed." The officer sat beside Hannah. "Cashman says you're a musician. I never learned to play an instrument."

Hannah felt warmth build inside her until it emerged as a smile. "You should have. Music makes it all worthwhile."

The officer asked if she was safe at home, but Hannah couldn't figure out any longer what "safe" even meant if her stepfather had been tracking her every movement for the last ten months.

Oh, crud, she wasn't safe. Did her stepfather have sniffers on the home Wi-Fi? Hannah would just have to use the network at the music school after the Thursday night practice to do the second set of changes.

It was a wonder the man hadn't died of boredom. Hannah worked days at the Brighthead Veterinary Clinic, with the occasional Saturday or Sunday at the regional emergency animal hospital. Tuesday and Thursday evenings were for rehearsal over at the Castleton School of Music. Weekends during this summer and fall had been scheduled to within an inch of their lives with weddings, music festivals, and dinner parties. She didn't socialize much. If Tyler wanted to find her (and if she wasn't working), then she was right on the other side of his living room wall.

If she'd had a cadre of hot boyfriends to send nude photos, she could understand why a man might want to hack her account. (He was her stepfather, so—gross. But he was still a man.) Instead, Hannah's mother needed her to take care of the little kids. Mom dreaded the day Hannah would fall in love, get married, and move out. "I'll lose you," Mom would frequently sob. Moving out would break her mother's heart, so Hannah stuck close to home. She'd helped after Parker was born, ten years younger than she was. Then when her stepdad came into the picture, she'd helped first with Bentley and next with Carter.

Was her stepfather trying to protect her? Hannah knew she was naive. Tyler said she'd never know if a guy was trying to take advantage of her, so maybe he was screening her email and texts to make sure no one would prey on her.

The detective said, "I may have to turn this over to the

state's cybercrimes unit. Our department is small, and so is Hartwell's. We're pretty solid on littering and noise violations, but not illegal monitoring software."

After the officer left, Cashman said, "I'll try with your phone and let you know if I can wipe it. If I were you, though, I'd take me up on the offer to trade phones and take cash for the difference."

Hannah frowned. "Doesn't that leave you with a dangerous phone?"

Cashman shrugged. "It won't be dangerous when I'm done with it. I'll take it apart and use the pieces to repair other phones. If there's anything dangerous, it's in memory, not in the battery or the camera or the screen."

Hannah said, "Should I assume he's got access to everything I send over the Wi-Fi at their house?"

Cashman huffed. "For now, assume he can. Assume he's got cameras in your apartment as well."

Her stomach heaved. "Oh my gosh."

"I'll send you an article on how to spot a hidden camera using your phone." Cashman looked worried. "Maybe you can find another place to stay?"

Hannah's heart dropped. She couldn't abandon her mother. "I don't know." The cat jumped onto the edge of the couch and glared at Hannah. Cats were refreshingly honest when they surveilled you, so she extended a hand to him. "I like your cat. He brooks no nonsense."

Cashman turned away. "He's not really my cat. He's a stray who comes in and out."

"Even so." The cat sniffed her hand and then withdrew, annoyed. "I'm sorry. I kept you here way late."

Cashman smirked at Hannah over his shoulder. "If it makes you feel less guilty, tell yourself I'm scoring major points with my wife by doing the right thing rather than pretending a factory reset would make everything fine."

She stretched further and managed to pet the cat's head. He slitted his eyes at her and looked pleased.

Cashman sighed. "Typical. If I reach for him, he gives me a nasty look."

She got to her feet. "I'll pay what I owe so far, and we can talk later about what to do with the actual phone."

Five minutes later, she was on Route 188 heading back to Hartwell.

Her stepfather was spying on her.

What would Tyler do when he realized she'd found the app?

What would Tyler do if the cops talked to him? What would he do to her mother? What would he do to the younger ones?

That was the worst question. The younger ones—they'd be completely at that man's mercy.

No, that wasn't the worst question. The worst question was whether Hannah's mother knew.

Even though she didn't have an exciting life, Hannah had never felt alone in the world. Not until now.

CHAPTER TWO

"Mr. Almendarez!" One of the students raced up to Enrique in the high school hallway. "Were you singing at a wedding last weekend in Bar Harbor? Because my mother totally thinks you were singing at the wedding."

Enrique raised his eyebrows. "That depends. Did she like how I sang?"

The student rolled her eyes. "Seriously? I'm going to take that as a yes."

"There were a lot of weddings in Bar Harbor last weekend. As it turns out, I did sing at one of them."

"See?" She flung up her hands. "Anyhow, she's got pictures if you want."

Enrique turned in at the chorus room where twenty students milled around their desks. It was a Friday afternoon, and based on the volume of their chatter, none of those students wanted to be here. He clapped his hands twice. "Let's get started! The winter concert is in eight weeks, and that Mozart piece is a disaster."

Speaking of disasters, a chorus with seventeen girls and only two guys was right up there. He'd manage. He'd managed last year with the same proportions and fewer students. The year before that had been his first year teaching, and then...well, he hadn't exactly *managed*, but at least he'd kept his job.

Sometimes Enrique thought of Vivaldi, and how he composed any number of bizarre instrumentations because his students arrived with whatever instrument they'd had at home. If Vivaldi had a bassoon, two cellos, a trumpet, and a harpsichordist, well, that's what he had. Enrique would just have to manage with seven sopranos, ten altos, and two tenors.

Mozart sounded good no matter what you were doing. In translation? Sure. With a million female voices drowning out the guys? Even so. With two guys who always looked kind of awkward on stage? That too.

Crawling through it one phrase at a time? That was undiluted pain.

The high school chorus's standards were above the middle school's. Two years ago, all these students were singing "Winter Wonderland" in unison and doing an okay job. Five years ago, these same students had been singing "Santa Claus is Coming to Town"...and it hadn't been great then either.

To be fair, the Mozart was the most difficult piece of the concert. The students had picked a number of other pieces to work on, some pop music, some standards, one piece from *Hamilton*, one from *Les Miz*. They'd fill their forty-five-minute slot and then file off the stage, and then Enrique could brace himself for the middle school concert the next night.

Followed by, heaven help him, the grammar school performances. The kids were cute, and they were enthusiastic. By the time he got through with them, though, he'd be ready for a long winter's nap.

With five minutes remaining until the bell, Enrique

talked to his students about dynamics and how the pieces would fit in with one another. "Remember, we've scheduled each piece in a specific order so the audience will experience a series of emotions that build from one song to the next. We're constructing a fictional world for them, some of it brutal, some of it gentle, and ending the evening feeling victorious. Next week, I'll be choosing soloists, so if you want to be considered, let me know."

One of the students raised her hand. "Go ahead, Miranda."

Miranda said, "At the National Honor Society meeting, they said we all need a ton of service hours, and I was wondering if the chorus could do something that gave us service hours too. Like if we could record our performance and send the video over to a hospital to make people happy."

Enrique was a very smart man with a great many proficiencies. Specifically, he was proficient at hearing students slithering out of doing real work. Not that many years ago, he'd been the evasive student. Arms folded, he said, "That's a good impulse. Music and live performances work together to raise people's spirits. Would there be general interest in doing some kind of community service?"

The students, all of whom would love to score an easy handful of hours, agreed wholeheartedly that they craved nothing more than to share the joy of song.

"A video isn't live music, though." Enrique paced the front of the room. "It seems to me we should take our song lineup and actually perform at the nursing home downtown, and maybe also the rehab hospital if they'll have us."

A few faces went blank, but other students sat forward. One said, "Like caroling! There's another nursing home like ten miles away where my grandmother is."

Another student raised his hand. "There's the children's home, too. The sophomore class is collecting toys for them anyhow, so what if we gave a concert when we delivered the toys?"

Enrique pointed at him. "I like how you think. What else?"

One of the girls said, "We could sing in front of the grocery store and have a kettle for people to donate money."

Her friend said, "If they donate enough, we stop singing?" and snickers filled the room.

"Collecting money may get us in trouble with the police." The bell rang, and Enrique raised his voice over the noise as the students started grabbing their bags. "Think of other public service ideas, and we'll talk about it on Monday!"

They were good kids. Their hearts were in the right places, and even though he thought he knew what to expect, sometimes they surprised him.

In the break room, Enrique checked his phone messages and found two texts from Hannah Staples. "Remember we've got a wedding together tonight. See you there!"

Followed by, "I knew you remembered. But Lindsey and Ashlyn were bugging me to send you the playlist again just so we don't have a hilarious mishap."

Fortunately for him, the song list she attached looked very much like the song list he'd prepared. Enrique replied, "Thanks. I don't want a hilarious mishap either."

Enrique liked performing with the Castleton String Quartet. Of all his backup musicians, they understood best how to calibrate their dynamics for a vocalist, as opposed to drowning him out, competing with him, not taking his cues, or changing the tempo on a song because that's what they'd always done. Even though half the players had changed this year, he and they never even practiced together any longer unless a bride wanted an exceptionally difficult piece, which was more than a small shame given how much fun they were.

Or rather, how much fun they used to be. Nearly a year ago, Bob Castleton had stepped down as first violinist when he'd been diagnosed with early-onset frontotemporal dementia. The FTD had destroyed his fine motor coordination, his memory, and his ability to speak. Enrique had stood by in horror while one of the finest musicians he'd ever known had tumbled into intellectual freefall.

After that, the quartet's lineup had changed. Lindsey Castleton had stepped up from second violinist to first violinist. Jason Woodward had come back from wherever he'd gone to make a name for himself, and now he played second violin. Ashlyn Merritt had previously been the violist, and there she stayed. Hannah Staples, whom Enrique had known for years, had left a local orchestra to come onboard full time as the cellist.

Knowing Hannah for years wasn't an anomaly. Robert and Susan Castleton's music school had turned out most of the musicians in the area. For anyone Enrique performed with, it wasn't a question of whether they'd gone through that school, but when and for how long. Enrique had started voice lessons at age six, but he'd also taken piano so he could accompany himself (and, later on, the chorus students). Hannah had taken voice only briefly. Her one-and-only love was the cello.

Hannah never hung out with their friends and never dated. She really did act as though she loved only her cello, and the cello loved her back, and that was the only relationship she'd need. It was kind of a shame, but Enrique had come to accept that the same way he accepted most of the other musical community's quirks. Hannah didn't stand out, didn't stand up, didn't speak up, didn't back out of anything she'd agreed to do. When he was with her, he knew what to expect.

Having Hannah in the quartet rather than as a backup meant they were interacting a lot more often, and that was pleasant. Hannah had a sense of humor. She had a sweet smile. She observed everything and then quietly made adjustments. In other words, she made for great accompaniment. Both musically and personally.

He texted, "Do you want to ride there together?"

She replied, "Sounds good. Should I bring anything other than gas money?"

He smiled at the phone. She was so tentative, so awkward. "Just conversation. It'll be a longish ride, and we can keep each other entertained."

CHAPTER THREE

On Friday afternoon, while Hannah was still getting used to her new phone, she got a security alert from her email account letting her know someone in Hartwell had attempted to login but had been blocked.

In the break room of the veterinary clinic, she sat dizzy at the table while the blood drained from her head.

Tyler must have realized that she'd found his spyware. After nearly twenty-four hours, he'd tried to peek at her email, discovered he was logged out, and attempted to log back in.

So much for thinking it might be a passive thing. Ever since yesterday, Hannah's hope had been that the phone just...well, just had weird stuff on it. Maybe Tyler hadn't realized. Maybe before slipping the phone into her Christmas stocking, he'd installed the spyware without planning to use it, in case one day Hannah bought fifteen guns and launched a bank-robbing road trip across

America's heartland. Maybe he'd done it to keep her mother happy but would never consider accessing her data.

Well, that would have been nice. Most fantasies were.

In Cashman's repair shop, the phone was doubtless taking pictures of the inside of a locked safe, assuming Cashman hadn't already parted the unit's guts out into ten different plastic baggies.

What would her stepfather do next? Finding himself locked out, he might go about his daily business figuring eventually the spyware would alert him to her new password. Or, alternatively, he might login to whatever site was collecting the data and discover that for the past twenty hours, it hadn't collected any at all.

She looked at her hands. Shaking. No good. She had another hour of work before she needed to drive nearly to Bangor with Enrique to play an evening wedding. No good, no good, no good.

Instead she called Cashman. "Did you figure out anything else about the phone?"

"I've been examining how it's gathering data, and I have to say, there are some scary people in the world. This software package touts itself as allowing parents to monitor their children's online presence, which is how they're getting away with this in the first place." He sighed. "The longer I search, the more I doubt I can scrub the phone."

Hannah said, "I just got a security alert that someone tried to login to my email account."

"Do you have the direct number for the Brighthead police?"

Hannah slumped at the table. "I just... I don't know if I want them to get involved."

"It's your call—well, it's literally your call, but I mean, more than that. You're the only one who knows if a visit from the police will escalate the situation or if you should wait until the cops can take him out of the house in handcuffs."

Hannah said, "I can't do that to my mother."

Cashman paused. At last, he said, "I don't know your family dynamics."

It would be too complicated to explain. Too much to talk about how Hannah's father had died when she was little, and how her mother got stuck with Parker after a man lit out on them. Then her stepfather showed up six years ago, but Mom had never gotten over losing two men. Mom's mantra was, "All I have is you."

"All I have is you," and it would be true in a ghastly way if Hannah got her stepfather arrested. Even if Hannah didn't get the man arrested, what would it do to her mother to think the two people she loved most in the world were opposed to one another?

All Hannah said to Cashman was, "No, it's complicated."

"It always is." His voice went more into business mode. "Do yourself a favor and turn on two-factor authentication for every account you can, that way if your spy actually guesses your new password, he'll still get blocked unless he's in physical possession of your phone. Speaking of which, take your time letting me know what I should do with the old one. There's no rush."

Still unsettled, Hannah cleaned the kennels for the vet clinic's overnight guests, administered subcutaneous fluids for a cat with chronic kidney issues, and talked a nervous owner through the process of giving insulin injections to a dog. At four, she changed into her concert blacks and drove to Enrique's place.

Enrique was larger than life. In fourth grade, she'd heard him sing and immediately known he belonged in the spotlight. For years, she'd kept her eyes on him whenever he talked, whenever he moved, whenever he roughhoused with the other guys. He had square shoulders and a square jaw and bright eyes, and he had a way of looking right at you and...well, *seeing* you. He didn't just gloss over you—he actually noticed.

That last bit might be a problem tonight. Hannah hadn't considered the spyware issue when she'd agreed to ride in his car.

Well, nothing for it now. Besides, it hadn't really been her idea to text Enrique to "remind" him to show up at tonight's wedding. That had been Ashlyn, delegating the reminder text to Hannah even though in twenty years Enrique had never once needed a reminder about a performance.

Now she found herself parked in front of a three-story apartment building with the GPS voice assuring her, "Arrived at destination." Enrique lived behind one of those windows, but she'd never figured out which. "I'm here," she texted.

She got out of the car and straightened her dress, then opened the back door to remove her cello. A minute later, Enrique was alongside the car. "Looking good!" he said, as though he himself didn't look like a million bucks in his tuxedo.

"Thanks. It's the splash of color that does it for me." Black was a color, right? "You ready for me and my fellow passenger?"

"Sure, although I have no idea how you haul this around on a regular basis."

Hannah rolled her eyes. "A cello weighs twenty pounds. You probably carry more than that up the stairs when you buy groceries."

Enrique reached around her to grab her backpack with the sheet music. "Especially when I carry all fifteen bags at once to save a trip. It's the cello's size that's the issue. Plus, two gallons of milk don't have a wooden bridge that could collapse."

"You're being overly technical." She shut the car door. "You don't have to carry my backpack too."

He grinned, and once again he looked amazing. "I'd rather be of service."

She followed him to his car, which barely accepted the cello in the back.

"Plenty of time." Enrique checked his GPS. "Do you remember Bob Castleton's first lesson about how to perform for public events?"

"Double the time you think it should take to travel and then add fifteen percent?" Hannah sighed as he pulled out onto the road. The fact that the same man had trained all of them made it even more ridiculous that Ashlyn had badgered Hannah to text Enrique a *reminder.* "'Early is on time, and on time is late.' That's saved my bacon a few times."

Enrique glanced at her. "You too?"

"Tourist season plus a major traffic accident. I was tempted to tune the cello in the car because we were stuck so long." Hannah shook her head. "Then it turned out a truck had overturned and three people had died, so I couldn't even complain. When I arrived at the wedding, everyone else was there except for the bride, who I guess had wanted to make a dramatic entrance at the stroke of twelve and instead arrived at the stroke of twelve fifty-two."

Enrique chuckled. "Saved in more ways than one."

"Yeah, that would be a funny story except for people dying. Sorry, I always come up with these grim scenarios." Hannah was good at changing the subject, since she always ruined the one they were on. "Okay, explain this: why would anyone come up to Maine for leaf-peeping season to hold their wedding at a resort known for its beautiful foliage, and then schedule the wedding for seven p.m. after the sun has gone down and no one gets to see the fall colors?"

Enrique added, "The fall colors they're being charged a premium to enjoy. I bet the morning weddings and the early-afternoon weddings cost three times as much, so the bridal party had their photo shoot six hours ago."

Hannah shook her head. "If you're going that route, you might as well take your pictures in front of a green screen and add the background later."

Enrique laughed louder and harder than she expected. "No, wait," he said as they pulled up at a light. "Wait, you need to see this. Picture day was last week." He poked madly at his phone, looking up at the light every couple of seconds, then tossed it into her lap as the light turned green. In the photo was Enrique in a tie—and no body.

"What—?" Then Hannah put it together and laughed just as hard as him. "You were wearing a green shirt?"

"And the software totally blended me into the artificial background. But look carefully because you can see my buttons hovering in midair."

Every time Hannah looked at the photo, it got funnier. Enrique said, "They want me to retake it, and I'm refusing unless they give me a printed copy of the original because I have to have that."

"Can I forward it to myself? Because suddenly I need to have it too." Hannah looked at it again, Enrique's floating head with his winning smile, his tie, his buttons—and the rest of him leaves and branches as though he were a woodland elf haunting his own forest. "Hey! Don't drive off the road!"

Enrique swiped tears from his eyes. "Next year they're going to send notices about not wearing green. I may wear the same shirt anyhow, just because."

"I stand corrected." The image flew a thousand miles from Enrique's phone to a satellite so it could get rebounded a thousand miles to the phone sitting in Hannah's lap, six inches from the originating device. "Wedding parties should not have their photos taken in front of a green screen."

She replaced his phone on the console, then checked hers to make sure the photo had arrived. It had. Also arriving was another security alert, this one from the bank.

She groaned. Nothing good was going to come of this. Nothing.

Enrique glanced at her. "Something wrong?"

Only everything. Only her stepfather discovering the death of the spyware. Only Hannah being so flighty that her stepfather needed to make sure she didn't abandon all her responsibilities. Only the sheer unbridled shame that she was apparently no better than a child who needed to be babysat.

Tears came to her eyes, and she stared out the passenger window. "It's just some stuff going on. It'll be okay."

In a soft voice, Enrique prompted, "You don't sound okay."

She very nearly told him she'd euthanized a cat today, how they'd expected to extract a diseased tooth, and only when they got the cat anesthetized did they open its jaws to find tumors all over the roof of its mouth. The sentence even hovered in her head, perfectly-crafted. *"We brought the sleeping cat back to the owner to tell her, and she burst into tears. We put him down without waking him up again."*

Instead she powered off her phone, worried that the spyware might somehow have crawled into the new one too. Then, sentence by sentence, she told Enrique the whole story.

Five minutes later, Enrique wasn't asking any more questions and wasn't even looking at her. Shame burned in Hannah's eyes, and she wrapped her hands around one another.

"Should I text my mother?" Hannah swallowed. "In case he's told her I emptied out my bank account and I'm leaving the state?"

Enrique exclaimed, "What? After that whole story, *that's* what you're worried about?"

Hannah cringed. "What should I be worried about?"

"You should be worried about how creepy that whole situation is! You should be worried about why the police haven't already banged on the door and told him to keep his nasty eyes to himself." Enrique's hands were so tight on the wheel that his knuckles were bloodless. "That's got to violate nine laws. Seriously, Hannah. Call back that cop and have her go threaten him."

Hannah shrank into the seat. "Mom and Tyler are probably just worried about me."

"No." Enrique's brow furrowed. "Worry is when your mother tells you to text when you get there because it's snowing. This is pathological. He tried to hack your bank account."

"Maybe he wanted to see if I had emptied it out."

"Even if you emptied it out, so what?" Enrique turned to her, his face darker. "You're not fourteen years old. You have the legal right to do whatever you want with your income, and you have the right to drive where you want, live where you want, and associate with anyone you want."

"My mother needs me."

Enrique snorted. "Your mother and stepfather are two able-bodied adults who are perfectly capable of taking care of the two children they chose to have. You're not expected to raise them. And based on what I've heard about Parker, he doesn't need raising."

Hannah shook her head. "Yeah, he's really angry."

Enrique muttered, "Gee, I wonder why?"

She recoiled. "You're not being fair to my family. It's not easy for them."

Enrique rolled his eyes. "No one has it easy. That doesn't mean you break the law and hack people's bank accounts."

Hannah shook her head. "He's not hacking. He used my password."

Enrique flung one hand in the air. "What do you think hacking is? Did you give him permission to go into all those accounts? Or did he use whatever tools he could find to put together where you had accounts, decode your login names and passwords, and then log in without your permission?"

"But a hacker is like—would take the money, would send messages…?"

Enrique huffed. "Why are you so set on defending him? You just said you spent an hour changing every password and setting up a new email account because you didn't want him in those accounts. You downgraded your phone to be rid of the spyware. If you're going to defend him, why not give him free access? Write your passwords on an index card and tape it to your mother's fridge."

Hannah folded her arms. "Why are you so angry at him?"

"Why aren't you?"

"Because it's complicated. The boys are all going to grow up and go away, and my mother will have no one."

Enrique stared at the road until the engine noise was the only sound filling the car.

It sounded bad, and everyone was going to hear it the way Enrique did. The police already did. The computer repair guy did. What if her stepfather was only being overzealous about protecting her mother? Nothing is forever. Plus, Hannah could get taken advantage of by an unscrupulous guy.

The GPS told them to leave route 1A in two miles. Enrique spoke again, his voice lower. "What happens now that the guy realizes you've locked down your security?"

Hannah wove her fingers into one another. "I was hoping maybe he only had that thing on my phone in case I went missing so he could tell the cops where to hunt for my body."

"You live in a strangely dangerous world and fear all the wrong things." Enrique sounded mystified. "The next time you see the guy, he's going to be angry. He'll figure out other ways to keep tabs on you. He'll put a GPS tracker on your car. If you've got a home computer, you'll need to lock that down as well."

She did have a home computer, but it was password protected and had been since the day she took it out of the box. Herself. The computer had come straight from the store to her apartment and been in her possession the entire time between.

Enrique checked the mirrors. "Here's the thing. If the guy was just meddlesome, he'll be grumpy for a while. Not a big deal. If he's a danger, though, he's twice as dangerous now because he thinks you're escaping control."

Hannah looked at her lap.

Enrique flexed his hands on the wheel. "I'm scared for you. Let's say he wants to get back into one of your accounts. He clicks, 'Forgot my password.' They will ask him your security questions. What was the name of your first pet? Who is your favorite musician? Who was your best friend in grammar school?"

Hannah's eyes widened. "He might not know all that."

"If you were ever a dependent on his taxes, he'll know your social security number. He knows your birthday and your mother's maiden name. If he chooses to retaliate, he could make your life a nightmare. Oh, and you'll need to put a lock on your credit so he can't open a line in your name."

"You're assuming he's going to do something criminal."

Enrique choked on his next words, then corrected with, "Hannah, I swear, you're not getting it. He's already done something criminal. You need to protect yourself."

The GPS guided them now, and conversation ceased. It was just as well.

When Enrique got them to the church parking lot, none of the others were there yet. They headed inside, Enrique once again carrying Hannah's backpack. They greeted the minister and traded jokes with the wedding coordinator, whom Enrique seemed to have worked with before. Maybe the quartet had landed this gig because of him. Lindsey and Enrique recommended one another on a regular basis.

Lindsey should have been here by now. Hannah turned her phone back on to see if Lindsey or Ashlyn had texted. From Ashlyn: "We're about five minutes out. Don't panic."

No panic. Jason wasn't here yet either.

Hannah got an email and clicked it open without thinking.

"Password Reset Request."

Hannah turned her phone back off, sick to her stomach.

CHAPTER FOUR

When was the last time Enrique had been this enraged?

He remembered quite a few times he'd wanted to throttle people, but none quite like this. His helplessness only added to the anger, and it intensified every blasted time Hannah defended her family for doing the unconscionable.

Lindsey and Ashlyn arrived, and the wedding coordinator debated with Lindsey for a full five minutes about where the quartet should set up, a fight Lindsey escalated by using an ever-increasing vocabulary of musical terms. Then Jason Woodward strode into the church mid-argument and said, "Why is this even a debate? Anyone would see we need to set up here," and suddenly it was over.

Lindsey said to Enrique, "Jason starts arguments with me, but ends them with everyone else."

Enrique grinned. "The coordinator knew she was

outnumbered."

Lindsey rolled her eyes. "It's because Jason looks like a billionaire in his tuxedo. People stare at him and forget their own names."

Side-eyeing her, Jason said, "Except for you. You forget my name and call me all sorts of other stuff."

"I'm immune to billionaires because I know your personality, pretty boy." Lindsey smiled like ice. "Since you've chosen to arrive, shall we tune?"

Enrique never could settle on whether Jason and Lindsey actively hated one another or were still working on getting there. For her own part, Hannah looked uncomfortable. Ashlyn was ignoring them, which was also Enrique's tactic.

Enrique went into one of the back rooms to start vocal warmups while the quartet tuned in the nave. Even tuning, they sounded good. One of them began a scale that never seemed to end, and it crested at a note that should have shattered crystal before heading back down to notes Enrique could sing. Scuffling sounds as chairs shifted about, and then the scale again. This time the acoustics must have passed muster because things settled down. Enrique reviewed his music and tried not to think about Hannah.

Hannah...and Parker. Now that was an interesting angle. Parker wasn't one of Enrique's students, nor was the five-year-old who'd just entered kindergarten. As a teacher, though, Enrique was a mandatory reporter. He could call the Department of Children's Services and report the stepfather for red flag behavior. What, though? Hannah wasn't a minor, and there was no evidence the stepfather had done anything wrong to the boys.

Still, the hair stood on Enrique's neck when he thought about a stepfather reading his grown stepdaughter's email and accessing her bank account. Tracking her whereabouts. Taking photos with her camera.

What kind of slimy thing was the guy doing? Enrique had seen too many statistics about girls being molested or killed by their mother's boyfriends. He couldn't trust this guy had anyone's best interests at heart.

Half an hour before the ceremony should start, the quartet began playing. From the prep room, Enrique closed his eyes and listened to the four instruments' voices blending, separating, then recombining. The two violins and viola sang so boldly, but then came the cello with its heart-rending sweetness and its resonating darkness.

Hannah could make that instrument emote. She always had. For the first time, Enrique wondered where the emotion came from.

He left the prep room to sit in the second row. When the ceremony started, he'd be up front, seated with the lector, but for now he had a prime spot to watch and listen.

The quartet was smooth and awesome in so many ways, the constant glances at one another, one eye on the music and the other watching for the cues Lindsey sent while playing. They could adjust to one another as easily as your heartbeat adjusts to your breathing. Although they were seated, all four shifted as they played, gentle like a wind chime in an evening breeze. Even Hannah, with that cello upright in front of her heart, was able to move with the music, her expression changing as though she and the instrument were holding a dramatic conversation.

In the car she'd seemed vulnerable, but here she was strong. Here she had balance. Immersed in the music, Hannah became beautiful. Enrique had never noticed that before. He'd never paid attention.

Beautiful and innocent. It made him even angrier, thinking about some monster attempting to crawl into Hannah's head, into her privacy, into her life itself, to devour all the things that filled her with wonder. Was that why she always faded into the background? Get noticed, and you'd become prey.

Emotional camouflage. He'd heard of it as "the grey rock technique." In the presence of a predator, pretend to be a grey rock. No one notices a small grey rock.

The quartet ended their piece, and then the coordinator signaled them. Enrique took his place while Lindsey started the music for seating the mother of the groom, the mother of the bride, and then serenade in the bridesmaids and groomsmen. The groom and best man took places at the front. The maid of honor processed. The flower girl. And finally, the bride.

Through it all, Enrique's eyes kept getting drawn to Hannah. Enrique concentrated until he heard only the cello, and he thrilled with the vibrato and the resonance and the dusky tones.

When they stopped playing, Enrique was startled to find the bride already at the front and the minister beginning the ceremony. He'd never gotten distracted during a performance.

He looked again at Hannah. Never until now.

In the prep room after the ceremony, Enrique hung around with the quartet. The instruments went back into their cases and the sheet music back into its folders.

Enrique took a place near Hannah. "You sounded great," he said, eyes on her. Maybe she'd hear that it was singular, not plural. He wasn't sure how to handle this.

He'd just sat through an entire ceremony about love and meeting the right person, getting warmer inside the whole time. Then he'd had to stand periodically and sing about love. That wasn't doing anything toward regulating this wild feeling.

It was uncomfortable, but he liked it.

Was Hannah dating anyone?

Had she ever dated anyone? Not that he could remember. At events, she showed up on her own. There weren't people in the audience for her at performances. She'd borrowed his phone once to call for a ride home, only then his parents had driven her. Where was it, though...? Oakwood Street? Oakview? He couldn't remember.

Jason was wiping down his violin with a soft cloth. Lindsey said, "People don't even bathe with as much care as you clean your instrument."

Jason didn't look up. "I'm not sure if you're critiquing my violin or my hygiene, or if it's a fantastic double entendre where you're critiquing both at the same time."

Ashlyn's nose wrinkled. "Oh, I didn't need that mental image."

Lindsey recoiled. "No, neither did I. It's sweet how you treat your violin like a fragile puppy."

Jason muttered, "*Sweet* isn't the impression I got from you."

"Think whatever you want. You usually do." Someone knocked at the door. "Mr. Astor," Lindsey exclaimed, shaking hands with the father of the bride. "Your daughter looked gorgeous, and I've seen a lot of brides."

Enrique parsed that statement exactly the way Lindsey did not want the father of the bride to parse it: both halves completely true, but not related to one another. Lindsey had in fact seen many weddings, but she wasn't exactly saying this bride was the most beautiful.

The father of the bride thanked them all for a great job with the music, then passed out tips. Tips were always appreciated, of course, and this man handed them over by palming the folded-up bills to each of them during a handshake. Enrique always figured that was to hide how the client was tipping some less than others, but maybe it was an upper-class thing where you pretended not to be tipping at all. He wouldn't know.

Lindsey gave Mr. Astor another one of their business cards, and Enrique did the same, "Just in case anyone asks." Odds were Enrique wasn't named in the wedding program, although he'd seen a copy of Lindsey's boilerplate contract where she stipulated exactly that. *Music provided by the Castleton String Quartet.* Enrique ought to grab a copy of her contract and copy the language. Sometimes the program mentioned him anyhow. *Soloist: Enrique Almendarez.*

When Astor left, Lindsey stretched. "Anyone know a decent spot around here for dinner?"

Jason said, "There's a seafood place about three miles back on 1A. Get the lobster roll and avoid the clams no matter what."

Ashlyn looked up. "The shack that looks like it's about to collapse? Why would you ever have gone there?"

Jason laughed. "You don't eat the decor! The lobster is top notch. They're one of those hidden local treasures."

Lindsey made a sad face. "You're trying to murder me. Shellfish allergy."

Jason turned to her, frowning. "And they let you live in Maine anyhow?"

"I know, right? But at a seafood place, there's too much chance of cross-contamination."

Jason mimed a distressed face. "Well, I don't want a murder rap. There's a diner not much further where they sell five-napkin burgers guaranteed to ruin a white shirt."

Every one of them was wearing a white shirt. Enrique said, "Bottle of peroxide in the laundry?"

Jason gave him a thumbs up. "There are chicken fingers and fries for the truly fastidious."

Lindsey said, "Meaning you?"

Jason opened his hands. "Sometimes meaning me."

Enrique said, "That sounds good," glancing at Hannah. "Actually, since I'm your ride home, it's up to you."

Hannah brightened up. "I'm fine with that. As long as we don't have to eat the decor."

After the bridal limousines departed and the guests drifted off to the reception site, Jason gave them directions to the burger place, and they drove in convoy. Hannah was back in Enrique's car, and Enrique's heart was trilling.

Hannah was beautiful. How had he failed to notice this before? The softness of her brown hair, the sweetness of her eyes, the glow of her skin, the smoothness of her movements. Her flowing black skirt and trim white blouse showed off her reed-thin body. She wasn't wearing makeup other than a little color around her eyes.

Enrique had nothing intelligent to say. How do you ask "getting to know you" questions of someone you've known for eighteen years? "So, it turns out, I never really singled you out before, and now I'm thinking maybe you're more interesting than I realized...?" That wouldn't go over well. Neither would, "It occurred to me when I was thinking what a jerk your stepfather was, maybe we could spend more time together?"

On the other hand, she was just now looking at her phone. He said, "Any more break-in attempts?"

She bit her lip. "Maybe he gave up. Or maybe he actually has my passwords and he's not clicking the button for two-factor authentication." She put the phone back in her pocket. "I've been activating that in every single account since the computer guy suggested it."

Maybe the computer guy should also have suggested she call the FBI to fry the guy with space lasers.

"Are you safe at home?" Enrique asked.

She shrugged. "He's never come into my side of the house."

Oh, dear heaven. She lived in the same house? Free baby-sitting and constant surveillance? She needed to escape.

The five of them walked into the burger shack looking notably out of place: both guys in tuxedos, the three women in ankle-length black skirts and white blouses. A waitress gave them the side-eye and then seated them right in front where everyone could see that this roadside burger stand had gotten a massive upgrade in clientele. Jason asked if Meredith was on tonight, and the waitress happily turned over their table to a woman who bounced up to Jason and was delighted to meet the quartet, which with a glaring lack of math skills she counted Enrique a member of.

The burgers were, as promised, a messy extravaganza

that jeopardized any and all white clothing. "The lobster place would have given us bibs," Enrique remarked, and Hannah laughed. He'd managed to seat himself beside her, and with Ashlyn on his other side, Hannah was right up against him. Ashlyn actually seemed to be pushing him closer to Hannah, but he didn't mind. His nerves wanted to crawl out of his skin toward her, and it didn't help matters that as the meal went on, all five began shedding clothing. Off came the tuxedo jackets and the ties. Everyone rolled up their sleeves. Lindsey was wearing a white tank top under her blouse, and if Ashlyn was to be believed, probably bike shorts under her skirt. He could imagine Hannah's body heat right next to him, and every so often, her arm brushed his.

Please, let them stay for dessert.

Fortunately, no one was in a mood to leave. Meredith kept swinging by the table to trade jabs with Jason, and Enrique grabbed a menu off the table behind to look at the desserts. "Ice cream," he suggested, which led to a groan from Ashlyn. Jason pointed out that none of the desserts involved shellfish, and Lindsey retorted that she had a perfectly-working steak knife at her disposal right here, thanks. Meredith cajoled them that if they wanted to stay longer, dessert was the way to convince the manager they weren't just squatting at a table.

Jason said, "Then I'd better get a brownie sundae," and Ashlyn convinced Lindsey to share a cheesecake slice.

Then Ashlyn turned to Enrique with mischievous eyes. "That leaves you and Hannah to share something sweet."

Feeling adventurous, Enrique said to Hannah, "Do you want to split an apple crisp?"

It mustn't have occurred to Hannah that this was a risky move on his part because she beamed. "Sounds great!"

So strange, noticing her all at once. On the one hand he felt like an idiot for not having registered just how feminine she was, but on the other hand, it was like walking into a roadside burger stand and encountering a world-class meal. Surprising, but in the best way possible.

CHAPTER FIVE

When Hannah got home, all the lights were on even though the little ones should have been in bed and asleep. About to park in the driveway, she shivered.

Lights. Her lights. The lights in her apartment were all on.

Hannah didn't turn in at her driveway. She let off the brake and kept rolling past the house, then rounded the corner before pulling up to the curb. She idled with her headlights off, but shutting off the engine felt like a terrible idea.

Anxious, she flexed her fingers into one another and struggled to breathe. Enrique had asked if her apartment was safe, and until this minute, she'd never thought it wasn't. In all these years, no one had made it unsafe. She had a lock on her apartment door, and no one had ever come in on her. Well, other than her mother bringing the kids on Saturday mornings so they didn't disturb Tyler.

That was understandable. No one went in when she wasn't there.

Had she left her lights on? She never did. Lights-off was one of those things Mom had drilled into Hannah from the time she was tiny: when there's no money, you don't give it all to the electric company. By accident Hannah might have left on one light, but all of them?

Her phone had fallen to the bottom of her backpack, and Hannah struggled to remember the new passcode. It had been off since before they'd gone to dinner with Enrique.

Enrique was so sweet. He'd made sure Hannah got half of everything, and when there was only one bite of apple crisp left, and one smidge of ice cream, he'd told her to finish it off. He was thoughtful that way. But then again, he always had been. Polite, that was. Polite and thoughtful. He treated everyone with respect.

The phone unlocked and yielded a dozen texts from her mother. The last was, "Hannah, call me now."

About to hit the button to call back, Hannah stopped herself. Better get information first. She scrolled through the messages and went cold, cold, cold.

The police had come.

Her mother was livid.

Her stepfather was outraged.

Now her mother was concerned.

Next message: questions from her mother as to what had gotten into her.

Meanwhile, Hannah had been at a burger shack in the middle of nowhere, perfectly safe, wedged into a booth with the people she trusted most in the world. While her family had been in chaos, she'd blown through tonight's tip on an amazing burger and a pile of fries the size of her head, plus a cherry-lime rickey and half an apple crisp. She should have been home.

Her mother was freaking out: had Hannah gotten in trouble with the police? Was she arrested? Was she dead? Why wasn't her location turned on?

Wait, what? Her mother had no reason to believe location services should be turned on unless Tyler had been telling Mom all along where she was.

Or if Mom had been accessing the spy data directly. Did no one trust her? Was Hannah so flighty that even her own mother assumed she'd abandon the family?

Still, the cops had come, and now her apartment's lights were on.

Hannah put the car in drive and circled the block. She'd have to face her mother sometime.

She made a second pass by the house, and this time at the corner, she didn't stop.

No, she would not go home. She should go to the police station and ask why they'd followed up on something Hannah hadn't even decided to press charges about. Then her mother would see it was all okay. Hannah could even blame some unnamed computer repair shop (except she'd made a call to Cashman Lavera on the phone before the spyware was off, so maybe they'd take it out on him?) and the trouble would be over. The cops wouldn't come again. Her mother would calm down. Maybe Hannah could install location services on the new phone just to keep her mother at ease.

She turned, then turned again, until she ended up on Farm Street.

Where could she go? Ashlyn and Lindsey shared an apartment, but she wasn't sure where. Jason didn't even live in Hartwell as far as she knew. She did know where Enrique lived, but that would be uncomfortable. "Hi, so remember what we were talking about? I was wondering if I could sleep on your couch." Plus, once her mother found out Hannah had spent the night in a man's apartment, the mistrust would never end. Spending the night meant finding new loyalties and leaving your old family. Her mother would never trust her again.

The only place Hannah could think of was a house she'd been in and out of all through childhood but hadn't visited in eight months, not since she'd been invited for dinner and been asked to take a full-time position in the Castleton String Quartet.

Susan Castleton let Hannah and her cello inside as though it were perfectly normal for stray humans to wander onto her porch late on a Friday night. The cello went into the living room, and Hannah went into the kitchen.

"You look distressed." Susan hugged her. "You sound more than distressed. How about I make tea for us both while you tell me what's going on? I assume you need a place to stay for the night?"

"I don't know what I need."

"Peach honey tea, probably." A gentle smile lit Susan's dark brown eyes. "I'm going to assume lots of sugar too, but you get to put that in for yourself."

Hannah returned the smile, but she felt like shattering. "Thanks."

With the kettle on, Susan returned to the table. "What's going on?"

Hannah tried to explain, but everything was so much more complicated now than it had been even four hours ago in Enrique's car. Susan wasn't asking questions, just assembling the pieces. When Hannah got to the part about the cops, Susan's brow furrowed, but still she didn't interrupt.

The tea boiled, and Susan went to pour it. "The phone with you now is the clean phone?"

The other phone was dirty? "Yes."

"Then I'm going to tell you, as a mother, that there's no excuse for either of them to have done that to your phone, and even less excuse to have tried breaking into your accounts." Susan carried two mugs to the table. "You don't want to blame them for what they did, but at the very least, installing monitoring software was a tremendous error in judgment. In the best-case scenario, the police gave them a warning that doing so was illegal and they're not to do it again."

Hannah paid more attention to adding sugar and milk than anyone in the history of tea-making.

Susan sat back, looking serious. "My suggestion would be to text your mother saying that you're all right, but you're spending the night somewhere else until everyone has had a chance to calm down."

Hannah bit her lip.

Susan said, "All the lights on? Including the lights in your apartment? What were they looking for?"

"Could the police have raided my apartment?"

"Not without a warrant. In fact," Susan added with a bitter tone, "I would bet your stepfather is the last person to let law enforcement search his home without a warrant. What he did to your phone is something the FBI would not be allowed to do without the signature of a judge, and they'd only get that with probable cause."

Confused, Hannah shrugged.

"Text her that you'll be back tomorrow afternoon. That should give her time to see reason."

Hannah said, "My mother is worried that I'll leave her. Staying away isn't going to help."

Susan sipped her tea. "Sweetie, the purpose of raising children is to enable them to leave. When they leave you, that's when you know you did your job right. Children aren't supposed to stay forever."

"She needs me to help with the little ones."

Susan's face tensed. "Did she ask you for permission to have them? Why are they your responsibility? Why isn't your stepfather helping with them?"

Hannah sighed. "I've defended my mother all day. I'm just so tired."

"All the more reason not to go back. Do you want me to do it for you?"

Hannah's eyes widened. "You— As if you're me?" When

Susan nodded, Hannah said, "But shouldn't I call?"

"If you call, she'll badger you into going home."

Hannah's shoulders dropped.

"Finish your tea. Text her. I'll put you up in Lindsey's old room." Susan offered a smile. "If you feel awkward about that, I'll invite Lindsey and Ashlyn over so it feels like a sleepover party."

Surprised into laughing, Hannah said, "I never did sleepovers as a kid."

"Then that settles it. Popcorn. Movies. Lots of giggling until three o'clock in the morning when Mad Mom Castleton storms out of her bedroom like a raging beast and threatens everyone with death if they don't quiet down right this instant."

Hannah kept laughing. It was way too late for this. Her judgment was off, and Susan was right: her mother would be able to badger her into anything.

She turned her phone back on and texted. "I'm safe, but I'm sleeping over with some of my girlfriends. I'll talk to you tomorrow after my performance."

Hannah hit send. That should convince Mom there was no romance involved and her daughter was being reasonable.

Susan was texting Lindsey and Ashlyn. "I could invite Sierra here too, but she's got a gig until midnight."

"That's fine." Hannah resumed texting her mother. "I have no idea why the cops would have been there. I didn't tell them to go to you."

Her mother texted back, "Call me."

The phone rang in her hands. Before Hannah could react, Susan slipped it from her and pushed the button to send the call straight to voicemail. "May I?" she said, and when Hannah nodded, she texted a sentence, then shut down the phone.

Hannah cringed. "What did you send?"

"I told her, 'I love you, Mom, and I'll see you tomorrow.' Let her get a handle on herself." Susan paused. "Did you tell her where you were?"

"No, she'd already be here." When Susan huffed, Hannah added, "I'm sorry. I know she gets worked up. She loves me and doesn't want to lose me."

Susan only looked at her without replying.

CHAPTER SIX

In the Castleton living room, Hannah awoke in a sleeping bag on an air mattress. Lindsey was out cold on the pull-out couch, and Ashlyn lay directly on the floor in a nest of throw blankets. Brightness seeped through the window blinds, but the longer Hannah studied the light, the more she decided the light was at a steep enough angle that they must be far later than sunrise.

How late? They had a performance at noon. She reached for her phone to check the time.

9:45. She hadn't slept so long in ages. Usually by now her mother would have brought the little ones for minding or maybe breakfast. Nearly ten felt like the heart of luxury.

But not for long because up popped a barrage of text notifications. Sighing, Hannah turned the phone back off. The only thing that caught her eye was her brother's name. Parker. Why would her mother even be texting about Parker? Or was her mother sending her tickets for an around-the-world guilt trip? If Hannah checked, there might be texts about Bentley and Carter too, claiming the little boys spent the morning sobbing big tears into their breakfast cereal because they missed Hannah so much.

Whatever. Hannah wasn't going to solve everyone's problems before breakfast. Susan had said last night that if Hannah didn't keep her phone off, her mother would keep upping the ante until Hannah felt compelled to call her back. Everything would become an emergency, and the emergencies would require her intervention. Susan had kept a flat tone. "If it's that bad, your mother needs to dial 9-1-1 and get the fire department or an ambulance. If it's not that bad, she can handle it herself."

Susan was a mom too, but did Susan really understand? On the other hand, Hannah wanted to believe her mother would be okay overnight without her, and maybe calmer now that it was morning.

It felt better daydreaming about last night's wedding. Enrique had sounded so good. Hannah had worked with a number of local soloists, not to mention family members who really wanted to sing "I Can't Help Falling in Love with You" at their cousin's wedding (but shouldn't have). Enrique knew how to modulate his voice to sing well with a string quartet. When he sang with a pianist, he changed his phrasing and his tone. Once she'd even heard him with Corwin's alternative rock band, and he'd used a much harsher sound.

He wasn't harsh, though. At dinner afterward, he'd been funny and thoughtful and friendly. He hadn't badgered her again about the privacy issue. In the car, he'd asked for stories about her job and told her stories about his. She wouldn't mind performing with him more often. She'd snuck looks at him several times during the wedding, and a couple of times even caught him looking back at the quartet.

He had nice eyes and a nice voice and a nice laugh. Somehow that added up to more than "nice," though. Three times nice? Nice cubed?

Smiling, she let her sleepy brain linger back over the singer in his tuxedo who'd thought to carry her backpack.

Eventually Hannah left the cocoon of warmth created by the sleeping bag, first finding the bathroom, next finding the coffee maker. Susan had left a can of coffee beans alongside it, and there was a sticky note on the machine. "All set up. Just push the button."

Hannah pushed the button, then stood at the glass doors leading to the back deck.

Maine's autumns were so beautiful. After a summer as wet and cool as they'd enjoyed, the turning leaves rioted with even more mayhem than usual. Meanwhile the pines were lush with green and the deciduous firs were turning gold in patches before shedding needles in a thick carpet.

Maybe she'd take the little ones to the land trust preserve where they could scamper on a trail for a mile or so. Get the kids good and worn out so they'd nap, dreaming of orange squirrels and the voles that darted along the ground without seeming to move their legs at all.

Springs creaked in the living room, and Lindsey joined her. "That was fun. I had no idea you liked scary movies."

"I didn't know I liked them either." Hannah opened the cabinet Susan had gotten mugs from last night. "Thank you for staying over."

"No problem. The stuff with your phone is scary. How often do you think he turned on the mic and just listened to us at rehearsal?" Lindsey shuddered. "After we eat breakfast, or lunch, or whatever it is when you get up this late, I'll go with you to talk to them. You sounded like you could use some backup."

That wasn't necessary. Bringing more witnesses would only make her mother more crazed.

Lindsey pulled a double waffle iron out from under the counter. "Let's see if I remember how to do this."

Hannah said, "Should we wait for your mom to get up?"

"Oh, she'll have been at the school since seven-thirty. There's a toddler song and dance class right at eight." Hannah must have looked horrified because Lindsey added, "It's fine. She knew what she was doing when she went to bed at midnight. She can read a clock."

Susan must be exhausted. She'd probably have gone to bed about the same time Hannah rolled in, self-absorbed and blurting out all her problems. Then instead of telling Hannah to fend for herself, Susan had made tea, arranged a sleepover, facilitated a difficult conversation, and finally popped popcorn in a cast-iron skillet while Lindsey called out every single title in their movie collection.

Ashlyn appeared at the table, her blonde hair rumpled. "What time do we have to play at the Autumn Leaf Festival?"

Hannah said, "Noon."

Lindsey whipped up the waffle batter in a scarred Pyrex bowl. "I wasn't thinking about that. It's going to be rushed if we try to talk to your folks beforehand. Let's have breakfast, then go straight to the festival and talk to your mom afterward."

Ashlyn muttered, "Well, *I* thought of it. That's why we brought our concert blacks last night."

Hannah looked in the fridge for syrup and butter, milk or cream, and anything else that might work with breakfast. She got plates from the cabinets while Lindsey poured batter into the waffle irons and flipped them over.

The phone rested like a lump in the pocket of the hoodie Lindsey had dug from a closet for Hannah to sleep in. They'd acted as though it were the most natural thing in the world just to welcome someone who showed up unannounced and asked for safe harbor.

Would it have been dangerous to go home last night? Had Hannah put them to all that trouble for nothing?

Hannah left the phone off. She'd said she wouldn't call back until the afternoon.

"Will Enrique be at the Autumn Leaf Festival?" Lindsey said.

Ashlyn said, "Well I certainly hope so," in a way that drew Hannah up short.

Lindsey chuckled. Hannah wasn't sure what they were

on about. Ashlyn was dating that guy Michael, who was Lindsey's long-lost brother. Lindsey had briefly dated Enrique a thousand years ago, but they'd been friends ever since.

Ashlyn said in a leading tone, "Hannah could text him to ask."

Hannah said, "I don't want to turn on my phone."

Ashlyn recoiled. "Oh, right. Sorry. I forgot why we were here."

"Good job." Lindsey brought two Belgian waffles to the table on little plates. "If he's at the festival, we might as well meet up. He seemed to have a good time last night."

Hannah smiled. "You noticed that too?"

Ashlyn said, "If you noticed it, no one's going to contradict you."

Hannah buttered her waffle, wondering what that was supposed to mean. In-jokes always left Hannah feeling excluded. Lindsey and Ashlyn lived together, sure, but it still felt awkward when they left her out.

The waffle was good, as was the coffee. Lindsey returned to the table with two more, but those were for her. "I put in another set, so when that's up, you each get a hot waffle." She drowned her waffles in syrup. "Then we need to get moving. We'll take one car."

Ashlyn said, "Are we hanging out at the fair afterward?"

"I'll check the performance schedule. There might be some groups worth hearing." Lindsey kept glancing at the waffle irons, waiting for the red light. "And maybe Enrique is singing?"

Ashlyn said, "Hannah should text him…?"

Hannah sighed. For whatever reason, neither of them wanted to do it, and she was so tired of being the odd woman out. "Fine. I'll ask."

While Lindsey fetched the final two waffles, Hannah turned the phone back on. The text app showed fifteen messages from her mother.

Her ears rang, and she could barely read the words before her as she scrolled through everything her mother had sent. The rage, the desperation, the guilt, the demands.

Ashlyn said, "What's wrong?"

"Everything." Hannah's vision went spotty, and she felt about to pass out. "My stepfather and my younger brother both got arrested."

She'd still have to perform.

She did not text Enrique to find out if he'd be there.

She handed the phone to Ashlyn, who read the texts back to Lindsey.

Parker had flown into a rage at Tyler. He'd tried to destroy Tyler's car. The cops had arrested them both.

Mom wanted her home.

Now.

Across from Hannah, Lindsey sat with her fingers pressed to her temples and her gaze squarely on the table.

"Okay." Lindsey's voice was soft. "I can get one of our subs out to the fair in time. That's not a problem."

How could Lindsey even say that? This was a huge problem, and none of their subs would be free on no notice.

Ashlyn said, "I'll drive you home because you look in no condition to drive anywhere."

Hannah wrapped her arms around herself. "Susan said this would happen. She said my mother would amp up the situation to get me back no matter what it took. That's why I turned off the phone."

Lindsey's head snapped up. "Are you saying your mother instigated Parker to have a fight with your stepfather?"

Ashlyn shook her head. "That's bonkers. No one would do that."

"Maybe everyone went off because my mother got crazed." Mom always told Hannah not to get upset because it upset everyone else. Had Mom failed to take her own advice? "Doesn't matter. It's wicked close to page a substitute. It's only a half-hour set, and I forget the world when I'm playing."

Lindsey was studying her.

Hannah clasped her hands together. "You don't believe me. You think I'm going to mess up and tank our reputation."

"Actually, I do believe you, and that worries me more. I don't like it when I do what you're talking about, so why would I make you do it?" Lindsey rested her forehead back against her fingertips. "Okay, new plan. We'll play. You'll call your mother afterward as if you never turned on your phone until two o'clock. I'll be with you if you need an alibi."

Ashlyn exclaimed, "An alibi? Why does it matter where Hannah was?"

Hannah said, "Because she'll want to know."

Ashlyn rolled her eyes.

Hannah hunched her shoulders. "What's happening to Parker? What happens when they arrest someone?"

Lindsey shrugged. "I have no honest clue."

Ashlyn bit her lip. "They'll have to go in front of a judge, get charged with something, then get bail set or get released on their own recognizance. It depends on what Parker and Tyler did that got them arrested. Disorderly conduct? Probably a warning and they're released until they come back for a hearing. They live in the same place, so Tyler might be ordered not to go home until it gets in front of a judge."

Mom would be livid. Beyond livid.

Lindsey gulped down the last of her coffee. "We have a plan. First, we get dressed and drive out to the festival. One thing at a time. That's the only way this gets solved."

Ashlyn said, "Did anyone text Enrique?"

Hannah set her phone face-down on the table. "No. It doesn't matter now."

CHAPTER SEVEN

As the bell rang on Monday, Enrique called the high school chorus to attention, then had to do it again, then clapped twice for a pair of girls and one of the guys in the last row. "Perhaps you'd like to tell us what's so entertaining?" he said, projecting his voice right to the back.

The guy said, "We're talking about Parker Kenton."

Hannah's brother? Enrique waved him on. "And you're bringing enough to share?"

One of the girls said, "He totally got arrested this weekend, didn't you hear?"

Enrique's stomach clenched. "He what? How?"

"He set fire to his father's car or something? People were talking about it at church on Sunday, and it's like a major disaster because his mother doesn't even want him to come home."

Enrique said, "Okay, enough. No gossip." He grabbed one of the better students. "Miranda, lead the class in warmups. I'll be right back."

In the hallway, he unlocked the instrument room and shut himself inside, then dialed Hannah.

Answer, answer, answer—

"Hello...?"

She sounded tentative. Terrified.

"Hannah? It's Enrique."

"Oh! I didn't recognize your number. My contacts didn't make it to the new phone. I'm sorry." If he'd needed any confirmation that a bomb had gone off in her life, the break in her voice would have served. "I thought you were — Well, it doesn't matter."

"What happened with Parker?"

"I don't know. It's a mess. Should you even be talking to me? You're teaching."

"Should you be talking to me? You're prepping animals for surgery."

"No, I'm here." She sounded so uptight. "I don't know what to do. I can't go home. My mother kicked Parker out. They got into a fight, and Children's Services came. They say Parker tried to kill Tyler, but Parker says he only wanted to destroy his car."

Enrique checked his watch. "You're in town, though? I'll meet you for lunch. Can we talk then?"

"I don't know. Parker's in emergency foster care somewhere, and I'm supposed to be talking to a social worker. I thought that's who was calling."

"How's this? When you've talked to the social worker, text me. I have time between the middle school chorus and the grammar school, so we can grab lunch once you know what's going on."

"Okay. I'm sorry. Thank you."

She could barely talk. How could she make decisions in this state?

Enrique said, "It's okay. You'll get through this."

Hannah said, "I hope so. Thanks for calling."

It was such a sterile way to end the conversation, as if he were phoning from the newspaper to verify a change to her subscription. *You're discontinuing Sunday delivery? Don't you want the coupon sections? Okay, thanks for calling.*

The students had finished warming up, and Enrique tried to keep his head in the game. He turned off his phone and didn't check messages between classes. He had a job to do.

Hannah. *How did everything blow up so badly, so quickly?*

Two hours later, when he'd finished with the middle schoolers, then he checked messages. Hannah had texted, "I still haven't heard."

He texted, "Hartwell Diner? Fifteen minutes?"

She replied, "Sure. If I'm late, it's because the social worker called."

He sent, "Absolutely. I will wait."

Shortly they sat in a booth at the Hartwell Diner with its cheesy Roaring 20s themed menus, ordering whatever standard thing looked most comforting. Hannah asked for clam chowder. Enrique ordered a lobster roll and thought about Lindsey with her shellfish allergy.

Although pale, Hannah had dark circles under her reddened eyes. Was this her first meal in days? She kept shifting her weight in the seat, looking at her hands or out the window but never at him. He wanted to slip around to her side of the booth and hug her until she settled down, but that would have made her more agitated.

"This is what I've pieced together." Hannah swallowed hard. "Tyler was freaked out because of the cops. They went into my apartment and turned the place inside out looking for something, but I don't know what."

Enrique said, "The cops?"

"No, Tyler and my mother. Tyler started drinking, and he threatened to hunt me down, and then he left the house. Meanwhile my mother was screaming at Parker for yelling at Tyler for threatening to hurt me."

Enrique went cold. "Sounds like everyone could have used a breather."

"I don't even know why the cops talked to Tyler in the first place. I didn't ask to file charges." Hannah looked up, lost. Again, Enrique's arms ached. If he could just hug her, hug her, hug her. Let her shelter with him so just one time, maybe for the first time, someone could be strong for her.

"Anyhow..." Her voice broke. "Parker went out of the house, and I don't get what happened next because no one's clear. At some point, Parker saw the car back in the driveway, and he started whaling on it with Tyler's sledgehammer. He smashed the windshield and the hood and the side windows and the headlights—just going to town on it. But he didn't realize Tyler was still inside, sleeping it off. That's what Parker says. Tyler says Parker was trying to kill him."

Enrique's head dropped back against the back of the booth. "What a mess."

"Tyler doesn't want Parker in the house if Parker is going to murder him. The cops say Parker has to go home. Mom said Parker can't come home, so she demanded they do a mental health assessment. The mental health people say Parker's not a danger, but where does he go? He's not going to prison. He's not mentally ill, and even if he was, he's not threatening suicide, so they don't care."

Enrique flinched. "I've heard about other kids that happened to, only they did need care. They weren't actively suicidal with a plan, so the hospital sent them home until they got desperate enough that they did have a plan."

Hannah looked up. "I don't understand. Why aren't we helping people?"

"Not enough beds for juveniles." Enrique frowned. "I've heard awful things in the teacher break room. Is this what the social worker is going to talk to you about?"

"They have to talk to me because it sounds like I'm the only relative who'll talk to them. It's such a disaster. I won't go home because apparently my mom and stepfather did go through everything in my apartment. I'd never feel safe there again. My mother says this is all my fault, that if I hadn't gone to the cops, Tyler wouldn't have gotten so upset, and then everything would be fine."

Enrique waited. Then, "You realize she's not telling the truth, right?"

Hannah blinked hard. "She's exactly right. The reason this happened is the cops went and talked to him."

The maze of Hannah's justifications wasn't something Enrique would be able to tackle over a bowl of clam chowder, so he let that go. He did ask Hannah if she wanted some of his steak fries, thick potato wedges deep-fried to a greasy golden shell on the outside. She dunked one into her chowder, took a bite, then worked her way down the whole fry in the same manner. He'd never seen someone do that, and it was cute, so he offered her more.

What could he say that wasn't an outright condemnation of her mother? "Where are you staying?"

"Susan Castleton said to stay in her house until we figure things out." She looked up, eyes glistening. "Mom didn't want to lose me, but because she let Tyler put that software on my phone, she's going to lose me anyhow."

Enrique couldn't fight it anymore. "How would this situation look different if you didn't feel responsible for your mother's every single life choice? I'm just curious."

Hannah glared out the window at the parking lot.

The diner's manager popped over, Rosalind Ward from the music school. "Enrique! Hannah! Sorry, I was doing inventory and missed that you're here." She smiled from him to Hannah, then drew breath as she realized how upset Hannah looked.

"No problem," Enrique said. "I didn't even realize you were ignoring us."

Hannah forced a smile. "You're from Corwin's band, right?"

Enrique said, "And you're the one with the Edgar Chantz shrine?"

"That's totally Corwin." Rosalind laughed. "Before every practice, he thanks Edgar's old practice room for letting us use it."

After a couple minutes' more chit-chat, Rosalind was gone, having distracted Hannah from being angry at Enrique—so whatever he said next, he'd better not mention her mother again. "I'll gather a posse of friends, and we'll pack you up and move you out. That will keep your stepfather from pawing through the rest of your things."

She wove her fingers through one another. "I'm getting a restraining order against him, but even if I don't, the cops said I should move out because my mom and Tyler violated my privacy. I was living in the house, though, so I figure that gives them some right."

Enrique smoldered. "By contrast, my lease gives me twenty-four hours' notice if the landlord wants to enter."

"I know, you've said it all over and over and over again, how much you hate my entire family and you think they're a disgrace." Hannah whipped up her head, and Enrique flinched. Right, right: don't mention her mother. "You want to hold my stepfather to the same standards as a law enforcement agency and my mother to the standards of a homeowner's association. My stepfather is the devil and my mother is an enabler, and the rest of my family are no better than animals."

Enrique raised his hands. "Loud and clear. I'll back off."

"You're still thinking it."

As if thinking about her mother's reprehensible behavior was somehow worse than her mother behaving reprehensibly. How could Hannah have analyzed this situation and concluded the problem wasn't the crime, but rather the people calling it a crime?

Still, Hannah ate her clam chowder in small, slow swallows, as though each spoonful made her sick. Enrique couldn't let that go on. "Have you looked yet for apartments?" It was a safe enough subject change.

"How does that work? I go and ask for a room, and I write a huge check, and then I have an apartment?" She snickered. "Everyone else figured that out at age nineteen, but that wasn't my strong suit. I went to college nearby, and I stayed on campus except for the weekends. Do I need a lawyer to represent me at the closing?"

A closing? "There's no closing for a rental. The apartment office will run a background check and a credit check. You pay them first month's rent and a security deposit, and then they'll give you the keys."

Hannah relaxed. "That doesn't sound so bad."

Enrique pushed his fry plate toward her again. Hannah must have forgiven him because she did the soup-dunk thing once more. Enrique would have to try that sometime, just to see if it tasted okay. "There may be an open apartment in my building, if you want me to ask."

She looked up. "I feel so stupid. I'm a total newbie at all of this."

She was innocent. Not quite naive, but innocent. She knew bad things could happen, and she had a sense of how they happened, but without any of the details. He'd go with her to look at apartments, and he'd tell her to take photos before moving in so when she moved out, she could prove she hadn't damaged the place. He'd talk her through some of the finer points, like maybe she'd need renter's insurance to cover her cello.

Oh, wait a minute.

"Your cello?" Enrique tried to hide the worry. "Where is it?"

"Susan's keeping it. I'm so glad I didn't go home on Friday night. At least I can still play. I have one set of concert blacks too, and that's the backbone of what I need to earn money."

Enrique said, "Plus your car."

"True. My day job doesn't have much of a dress code, so that's a good thing."

Her phone rang, and she dropped her spoon as if she'd heard gunfire.

Enrique said, "If it's social work, take it."

Hannah was shaking. "Hello?"

Her side of the conversation wasn't a revelation, just a lot of "Yeah" and "Okay," but then it became, "I don't know if I could do that." Next, "You're right. But I don't know." Finally, "I don't have a place to live right now."

Enrique's hair was on end, and now he was paying attention because he could decode the other side of the conversation. The social worker was asking if Parker could live with Hannah. Or depending on how bad the situation was, maybe all three kids.

Hannah closed her eyes. "Can I talk to you in person? Can I see him?" A pause. "What does he want to do?"

Enrique held his breath.

"We'll figure it out. He may be able to stay with me where I am now. I'll have to ask." She bit her lip. "Okay. Thanks."

When she was off the phone, Enrique said, "Parker's going to live with you?"

She stared at the tabletop. "My mother won't let him back in the house."

"What about the other two kids?"

She shrugged. "They didn't do anything wrong."

Enrique only said, "I guess," rather than, "This isn't about punishing Parker."

Hannah looked so lost, so lost, so lost. Overwhelmed, she wasn't even sure where to start rebuilding her life.

Or building it. She'd never been allowed to chart her own course, and now not only was she having to do that, but also build her own boat and construct her own pier.

Before he thought twice, he reached across the table for her hand. "I promise, it's going to work out. You go see Parker first. That will steady you. You'll get a sense of what happens next and what kind of timeline you're working against. I've got to teach this afternoon, but I'll reach out to the apartment management, and I'll ask if anyone else I know has a place."

She didn't pull back, and he held tight because she was about to crumble. Beneath his hand, hers felt so small. Her voice, too, emerged small. "You're so confident it's going to work out. I don't see how."

CHAPTER EIGHT

En route to the social worker, Hannah called Susan, who answered with an all-business tone. "Okay, what's going on?"

"My mother refused to let Parker come home, but he's only fifteen, so they can't just kick him out. My mother is demanding the state take him. The state doesn't want him either, so they're talking about emergency protective custody."

Susan said, "I'm cleared with the state for emergency foster care. Give the social worker my name and tell her Parker can stay with me."

Hannah nearly drove into a tree. Ears ringing, she pulled across the neck of the nearest driveway.

"After Bob's diagnosis, I said we couldn't do it any longer, but this is the very definition of an emergency situation. You're already in my house, so it makes sense for Parker to come to us." Susan hesitated, and Hannah could practically hear her correcting herself: *"Not us. Me."*

Susan continued, "You're going to their offices? I'll meet you there. I may even know the social worker in charge of his case. It'll take me fifteen minutes."

Hannah said, "Where are you?"

"I'm at the hospital with Bob. It's fine."

Hannah's voice broke to a whisper. "Thank you."

She didn't put the car back in gear right away. She texted Enrique. "Susan says Parker and I can stay with her."

Susan was leaving her husband's side in order to come to Hannah's. Two families, both falling apart.

When the social worker and her brother entered the conference room, Hannah leaped from her chair and rushed Parker, hugging him as hard as she could.

He grumbled, "Quit it."

"Are you okay?" She backed off to arm's length but didn't let him go. "Did you get hurt?"

Parker spat, "I'm fine."

The social worker shifted a stack of folders to one arm so she could shake Hannah's hand, introducing herself as Caroline Lebak. "I'm really glad you could come right away. One of our goals is to keep families together as much as possible, so your help means a lot."

"We may have a place to stay, at least temporarily."

Parker exclaimed, "You can't go back there!"

"No, we can't." Hannah shivered. "Not after what they did, and what they said you did."

Parker looked deadly. "You'd have done it too. He was like a maniac threatening you, and I couldn't let him."

Caroline said to Hannah, "Parker says he destroyed Tyler's car to protect you."

Parker folded his arms. "Tyler said after he was done, you'd regret what you did. I didn't even get what was going on at first, but he was out of control. He said he'd track you down, so I made sure he couldn't get where you were."

Hannah bit her lip. "Did he hit you?"

"I didn't care if he hit me! Don't you get it?" Parker got right in her face. "He threatened to kill you!"

Hannah put her hand to her mouth. Ears ringing, she made her way to the nearest chair.

Kill her? Tyler said he'd kill her? For stripping his spyware off her phone? And her mother was defending him?

Susan entered, nodded at Caroline, and took a seat next to Hannah at the glossy table. Hannah's lips had gone numb.

Caroline said, "The situation is extremely complicated, and there's a lot to get through, so I'd like to get started, please."

Parker rolled his eyes, and Hannah grabbed his hand. "Let's do this stuff first. We'll figure out later what to do about Tyler. It's going to work out."

Enrique kept saying that. *It's going to work out.*

With Parker in the same room, this was the first time she felt like it would.

Susan started asking questions, and it sounded like she did know Caroline. Five minutes later, two other women entered the room, and Susan knew both of them too.

Hannah leaned over to Parker. "Susan Castleton is the owner of the music school. I've been staying with her. Her daughter runs my quartet."

Susan looked over to them. "It would be best if you two stay together. If that means you have me as an emergency guardian, then at least Hannah will be with you, too."

Hannah said, "He can go back to school?"

Susan nodded. "By keeping him in town, we'll minimize the disruption. He can be with his friends and keep up with his sports and other activities." She glanced at one of the other women. "Which, if you recall, is exactly the case I made about Ashlyn Merritt."

Ashlyn? Hannah hadn't realized Ashlyn went through this too, or that when Ashlyn was talking about the legal system, maybe she knew from experience.

The meeting went on forever. Hannah kept putting her hand on Parker, and Parker kept yanking away. She needed to feel him, though; needed to be sure. So much had fallen apart. But Parker was here.

Susan said, "I'm not sure why you're letting the two smaller children remain in the house."

Caroline shook her head. "The children aren't in immediate danger."

"Let's see." Susan folded her arms. "Coercive control over a grown adult stepdaughter. Threats against Hannah's well-being. Repeated multiple violations of privacy followed by vandalism. And then physical violence against the minor stepson."

"That won't get a judge to issue a protective custody order. There is no legal basis to assume the younger children are in danger." Caroline raised her hands. "I hate it just as much as you do."

Hannah said, "If you take the kids away from my mother, she'll die."

Susan's eyes narrowed. "Your mother isn't the primary concern in this discussion."

Hannah leaned forward. "But she *is* a primary concern. If you take everything away from her and leave her with nothing—"

"We're the Department of Children's Services, not the Department of Mother Services." Caroline glanced at her paperwork. "Regardless, we're not leaving her with nothing. The two youngest are staying, and Tyler is still in the home. Parker is our sole focus." She turned to Susan. "Because Hannah is an adult, the threats against her aren't a primary consideration in the case. Of course it matters, but if we go in front of a judge, we're only presenting facts the judge will listen to. It's best to concentrate right now on Parker and what will help him."

The first emergency hearing had resulted in Parker's removal from the home. There would be another hearing in the next few weeks, and after that, the team would come up with a set of conditions for reuniting Parker with Mom and Tyler.

Parker grunted. "Make sure there are a lot of conditions so I won't do any of them. I don't want to go back."

Caroline nodded. "Heard and noted. That's for our next meeting. At that point, we'll also come up with a schedule for visitation."

Susan said, "Supervised."

Caroline looked up, surprised. "Yes, of course."

Parker said, "You can set up visitation, but I'm not going. Mom chose Tyler. She doesn't get to choose me too. And she doesn't get Hannah."

Susan met Parker's eyes, and something passed between them. Susan looked like a military general planning a sortie—and Parker must have caught it because he straightened. Hannah knew that feeling, the moment you knew Susan had not only looked at you, but had seen you.

No one ever saw Hannah. She planned it that way. It was just easier, except for the moments it wasn't. Then Susan looked at you, saw you, and accepted you. All those things you thought would drive everyone away were fine with her, and in that moment, your guard came down.

Susan looked back to Caroline, steady. "The most important thing right now is whether Hannah becomes his guardian or I do. I'd prefer it be her, but they're both welcome in my house for as long as necessary."

Hannah huddled forward, face in her hands.

Susan said, "Over the long term, they'll need an apartment. Can you find them something, at least on an emergency basis? Also, Hannah needs a stipend so she can get whatever they'll need to live in it."

Unable to look up, Hannah swallowed hard. "Speaking of which, can I have a police escort? I need to get back into my apartment and take everything out of there."

Enrique had told her everything was going to work out, and Hannah wanted to believe him.

She had a team working with her now. The social workers had forms and routines, and Susan had experience. The team had a schedule, and they had the law at their back as well as a judge to interpret that law.

They had an appointment with the police to enter the house and reclaim whatever they could of Hannah's belongings and Parker's.

While the social workers were making copies, Hannah texted Enrique. "I think you're right. It may work out."

Then they discussed the legal issues. Parker was facing vandalism and assault charges.

"And Tyler doesn't face threatening or harassment charges?" Parker shouted. "How about spying on Hannah? He gets off free?"

Caroline shook her head. "He's being charged too. Like I said, this is an incredibly complicated situation, and we're tackling just one piece of it. It seems to you like we're ignoring him, but I promise there's another office in town where he's yelling at a public defender that they're blaming everything on him and letting you off the hook."

Susan gave Parker a dark smile, and again Parker seemed to get that she was on his side. She said, "Trust us that no one in this room thinks that man did anything right."

Hannah had no idea where to look, no idea what to do. For days now she'd been making excuses for the man. Here she was though, surrounded by professionals and people who cared, all of them saying the same thing Susan said: no one would justify what Tyler had done. Parker had gotten in trouble standing up for Hannah when she hadn't stood up for herself. She'd tried to wish everything away, and her inaction had made the whole situation explode.

Caroline said to Parker, "Right now, we are your defense. We're going to do our best to protect you. That's our only goal. Ideally, we would make your family function again, but if that's impossible, we'll get you as close to stable as we possibly can."

Hannah said, "As of now, I'm his family."

It would work out: but she'd have to be clear-eyed about doing the work.

CHAPTER NINE

Enrique showed up to Oakview Drive with his brother Daniel's pickup truck as well as his brother Daniel, plus Daniel's friend Ted. They barely fit across the front seat, and that was good. Daniel was no slim twig of a man, and Ted was a firefighter. When Enrique had offered the guy fifty bucks to stand around looking irritated, the guy jumped on it.

It was Monday night, and cars crowded the street around 29 Oakview. Two police cars, because the police in Hartwell were chronically bored. A Honda Pilot. A couple of cars Enrique didn't recognize. And now his brother's pickup.

"This is going to be fun," said Ted. "Do we have a list of the things we're retrieving?"

"She didn't give it to me." Enrique opened the door and slid out. "I just hope this goes smoothly."

His brother strode around the other side of the truck.

"And I hope it doesn't."

Daniel's wife had a son from a previous relationship, and when Daniel had heard what Hannah's stepfather had done to her phone, he'd raged. Seriously raged. "That's not what a stepfather does. That's not how you treat a stepkid, like she's a spy from the enemy. You want to do that garbage? You join the CIA. You want to be a kid's dad? You treat the kid with respect."

Enrique hadn't asked if Ted the firefighter had a dog in the fight, but it didn't matter. Ted also looked like he was hoping it didn't go smoothly, plus he knew the entire police department. As they walked toward the police cars, he greeted all three officers by name.

The air carried a chill of both impending winter and an impending fight. Enrique hoped the stepfather had opted not to be home. That would be easiest for everyone. Was the restraining order in place yet?

Hannah's car pulled up last, and she parked across the street. Their group was rather large, with Enrique's contingent plus the police, plus Lindsey and Susan, plus Parker and Hannah. While they gathered, the stepfather and two other guys came onto the porch, glowering with folded arms.

The police sergeant lowered his voice about half an octave and flattened out the tone so he was total business. "Hannah, you will be accompanied at all times by Officer Stevens. Parker, you will be with Officer Edwards. If you've got a list of your belongings and where you'll get them, give that list to Edwards. Because of the legal issues, you'll have to stick to the rooms where those items are located. I'll be with the homeowners outside the home while you're inside. If they attempt to talk to you, don't respond. Don't engage. Don't do a thing other than gather your belongings and get out of the house."

Parker said, "And if they broke all my stuff?"

The sergeant said, "If anything was vandalized, destroyed, or removed, report it immediately to Edwards. We'll photograph everything we can, but it's vital that you not get into a fight with them during the retrieval."

A fourth officer exited the house in the company of the stepfather and two other men. The sergeant went over to them, then returned. "Your mother is going to stay in her bedroom with the two youngest children so they aren't traumatized."

Parker gave a bitter laugh. "That's why Tyler invited two of his gangster friends over? So no one would be traumatized?"

Enrique said, "Perhaps there was a better way to make sure the little kids weren't traumatized. Like not engaging in this behavior in the first place."

Ted laughed. "You'd think, but that never occurs to these people."

The sergeant made a "tone it down" motion with his hands. "No one wants any trouble. You'll have to avoid the master bedroom, is all. If there's anything in there that you need, I will retrieve it afterward."

Enrique said, "They could be hiding anything in there."

"We'll handle it if it happens." The sergeant looked around. "You've got boxes?"

Susan said, "We're all set."

The sergeant's "no one wants any trouble" sounded to Enrique more like wishful thinking than reality. For one thing, Daniel wanted trouble. Hannah's stepfather looked like he wanted trouble too. As they walked in, Tyler shouted at Hannah, "You're breaking your mother's heart."

Parker shouted back, "Shut your stupid face."

Hannah grabbed his hand and hissed something at him. They went inside past Tyler's glaring eyes, and then they peeled off.

Hannah brought them to the in-law apartment, which looked like a sweet setup if you weren't co-existing with monsters. It was a narrow slice of a square New England home, ten feet wide with a combined kitchen/living room on the ground floor. A slim staircase led to a second floor, which must be her bedroom.

In the doorway, she stopped cold. "They trashed

everything," she whispered, then braced herself. "Well, that makes it easier. Shove everything into boxes or bags without worrying about packing nicely. I'll sort it all later."

Lindsey slipped past her. "Mom, you go upstairs with Hannah. Enrique, you and Daniel are going to pack everything out of the living room. I'll tackle the kitchenette. When you fill a box, write the room name on it and seal it up." She turned to the officer. "Please take photos to document because obviously she didn't leave it in this condition."

Edwards went upstairs with Hannah and Susan to photograph while Enrique shoveled books and DVDs into a box. Daniel ranted the whole time. "I hope that slime mold moves out of state because if they ever find him in a shallow grave, I want to be sure I didn't black out and do it myself."

Enrique stood books in the bottom of a box so he could get another layer. "He's not worth doing the time for."

"You say that, but the satisfaction…?"

Hannah was all business. The sun went down, and they were still working. Susan left with the firefighter and a Honda full of boxes. They started making up a second load, and when Susan returned, Enrique and Daniel carried out the futon.

The stepfather confronted them on the driveway. "That's not her furniture. I paid for that."

Daniel said, "You got receipts?"

"You can go hang. I know what I paid for."

Daniel said, "She says she bought it, so it's going in my truck, and you can take her to small claims court."

The officers consulted. Enrique went inside to find Hannah. She looked exhausted.

"Tyler wants to keep your furniture. He says he bought it."

Hannah closed her eyes. "He may have bought some of it. Most of it's just garage sale stuff. It's hardly worth fighting for."

Enrique said, "Would your mother remember?"

Susan strode into the room. "Her mother's not going to side against a vindictive man who's living in the same house." Susan sealed up a carton with packing tape and wrote "BATHROOM" across the top. "On the other hand, I'm feeling kind of vindictive myself, and I want to take every lightbulb and put eggs in all the radiators before we leave."

Hannah didn't even laugh. Enrique said, "Industry standard is raw chicken behind the baseboards. But I need to know what to tell them about the futon because he's arguing with Daniel."

Ted flexed his shoulders. "Then I'm definitely loading it in the pickup."

Hannah looked around. "The bed's theirs. The desk and the bookshelf too." Those were the style you'd have in a kid bedroom, so Enrique could believe that. "The kitchen table is his. The futon is mine. I bought the end tables. The lamp in here is from my mother, but the others are mine."

Susan said, "Tell him we're taking the futon. Grab this and that," she said, pointing to the end tables and the other lamps. "I'm carrying out the microwave. I need someone to take the toaster oven, and then we'll do one last pass."

Enrique said, "A lightbulb harvest?"

Susan's eyes darkened. "Maybe an egg hunt, too."

None of this was fair, and Enrique had no way to comfort Hannah about the unfairness.

Hannah huddled on Susan's couch, a mug of hot chocolate in her hands even though it must have been burning her palms. She hadn't drunk any of it in five minutes. "I don't even trust my stuff. There might be GPS trackers in everything."

Susan said, "There's some risk that he did that, but you can't go off the deep end."

Parker was in an easy chair in the corner, legs thrown over the arm rest, an empty mug within arm's reach. To Enrique, the scene felt familiar. After a competition or a state-level performance, Bob and Susan used to bring their students back to this house—this room—to unwind. Usually it had been Enrique on the easy chair with his legs over the arm.

Daniel and Ted had left. Lindsey was texting Ashlyn from the kitchen. Susan had seated herself on the floor near the unused fireplace.

Susan said, "You'll need to divert your mail. Anything that goes to their house, assume it's gone forever."

"I've already made everything paperless that can be." Hannah slackened into the couch. "There's so many things I need to take care of."

Enrique slid over next to her, and he took the mug from her hands. "Let me do you a favor." He set it aside, and then he hugged her.

She relaxed into him, and his heart melted. He'd have done anything in that moment to protect her from the million vital and impossible tasks confronting her.

With his arm around her shoulders, he squeezed her closer. "One thing at a time, we'll get it done."

"It all needs to be done yesterday."

"You've got time. No one's kicking you out of here." Susan turned to Parker. "I mean that. Tomorrow, you and I will hammer out some house rules so we know how not to get in each other's hair, and so you can come and go without anyone breathing down your neck."

Parker muttered, "Thank you," as if it were the most annoying thing in the world to have his wants acknowledged.

Hannah said, "We'll have to pay rent and food and stuff."

Susan said, "We'll work that out later," and Enrique thought she meant, "It's not really a big deal."

Lindsey returned to the living room. "I've got a couple hours in the middle of the day tomorrow when I could pre-screen apartments. I know you've got to work, so that saves you time."

Hannah tucked up her knees and pulled away from Enrique, but he didn't let her go. "I'm making all of this work for everyone else."

Enrique warmed with her against him. "We're fine with it. No one's making us do this."

Parker said, "And if Tyler does anything else, I'll kill him."

Susan sighed. "You will not kill him. If he does anything else, we will get him arrested. We may involve child protective services and get the younger kids removed, but we will not break the law."

Parker rolled his eyes.

Enrique said, "I get it. I'm furious too. Stay away from the guy anyway."

Parker snorted. "That's not exactly hard to do, since Mom kicked me out."

Enrique said, "Actually, Hannah, you'll need to file papers with the school to inform them you're now Parker's legal guardian, and that your parents aren't allowed to access information on him."

Hannah shuddered. "I'd better freeze Parker's credit, too. And lock his bank account. How are apartments going to do a credit check on me if everything's frozen?"

A timer went off in the kitchen, and both Lindsey and Susan got to their feet. "I've got this," Lindsey said, but Susan went with her anyhow.

Parker studied Enrique. "So, Mr. A? Why are you even here?"

Enrique said, "I was with Hannah the day she found out about the spyware."

Parker didn't let off the stare. "Can we move in with you?"

Hannah's head came up. "Parker, seriously?"

"It's a legit question. He's got his arms around you, and

he stared down Tyler in a face-off on the lawn." Parker folded his arms. "That looks like a boyfriend to me. Why don't we just move in with Mr. A?"

Enrique tensed.

Hannah said, "Because we're not dating, and even if we were, there's a huge jump from dating to living together."

Heart hammering, Enrique had no idea how to answer this. Although he didn't need to. Hannah was perfectly clear.

Except he wanted to say, "We *could* be dating."

Parker said, "If we lived with Mr. A, then you wouldn't have to worry about Tyler barging in on us."

As if Enrique would be able to beat up a guy who tossed around car parts for a living. Maybe he could sing the man to sleep.

Hannah said, "If Tyler comes to us, I'm calling the cops."

"Cops take like five minutes to get there. Tyler goes zero to sixty in five seconds." Parker looked at Enrique. "But you'd drive him off."

Enrique had his brother's height but not his brother's physique, let alone Ted's. Tyler would go through Enrique like a wall of tissue paper. "I'd get between you. He's not stupid, though. He wouldn't act like a brute if someone else were around."

Susan was setting the table. "It's a good point though that you might need an apartment building with two layers of security. Social work may have a lead on a place, since they keep telling me their whole thrust is to keep families together."

Parker said to Enrique, "What are you waiting for? Move her in, and that makes a family."

Hannah sighed. "No. That's how *Mom* makes a family. She jumped right into things with Tyler and then pretended it was a family." Hannah sat away from Enrique, but before she let go fully, she squeezed his hand and sent a jolt of lightning through his heart. "The right guy would be worth waiting for, and the right guy would want to grow a relationship slowly."

CHAPTER TEN

Hannah walked outside with Enrique while Lindsey finalized plans with her mother, after which she'd drive Enrique home. Parker was in the kitchen, very grudgingly drying the pots and pans as Susan washed.

"Parker helped out with Mom. He'll catch on here." Hannah sighed, but the discomfort lingered. "I'm sorry Parker was all over you to have us move into your apartment."

Her cheeks burned. She'd felt so good having Enrique's arms around her. For the last week, whenever she'd had no strength and seen no way forward, she'd been leaning into Enrique's assurances. When Parker called attention to it, though, the shame scorched through her. She had no right.

Enrique chuckled. "He thought we were dating, so it was a reasonable question."

He paused, then, and Hannah wondered if the subject made him just as uncomfortable as it made her.

She'd never had a real boyfriend. The purpose of dating was to get married, and it was understood that she couldn't marry. Mom was always on about, "Someday you'll have a kid of your own, and they'll be just as ungrateful as you are." Her mother had snapped it even when Hannah had been getting ready for prom. Her date was one of the quieter guys who'd mustered up the courage to ask Hannah out and then asked if she wanted flowers to match her dress. Her mother had said, "For years you sacrifice for your child, and then they abandon you."

Hannah's prom dress had been elegant, a cream dress with gold overlay. Her date had been timid with an understated sense of humor. She'd had a great time and then never gone out with him again.

Enrique lowered his voice. "You didn't mind that Parker thought we were dating?"

Hannah shifted uncomfortably. "Well, we're not."

His hand rested on her shoulder, and he came around in front of her. "There's a lot going on right now. But do you think maybe Parker saw something that could work?"

Hannah's brain spun. Was Enrique asking her to live with him? He had an apartment, and she needed an apartment—but that was crazy. How much did she know him?"

Enrique said, "Would it be all right if I took you out for dinner?"

Tense from head to toe, Hannah fought the urge to slink into the shadows. Dinner together wasn't moving in together. Dinner was just food, and they both needed to eat. Plus, it felt good to be with him. He left her feeling relaxed—feeling confident. She'd known him for ages, and she always enjoyed seeing him. Why not for dinner too? "That would be all right."

Enrique smiled, and he was gorgeous. As his eyes gazed into hers, warmth spread over her.

It made no sense, but it felt right. Actually, it felt amazing. He took her hand, and then she put her other hand on top of his on top of hers.

Enrique pitched his voice low, and the tone went right through her. "And if I hug you sometimes, even when you're not needing comfort—would that be all right too?"

The hair stood on end at the back of her neck. How far did he want to take this?

He squeezed her hand. "Okay, I'll back off. You're going through a lot, and I don't want to scare you. I'll text you tomorrow to check up, and we can schedule dinner then."

Their hands parted as Lindsey came out of the house. "You ready to go, Enrique?"

"Sure." Enrique smiled at Hannah. "Talk to you later."

"Yeah." The word nearly broke in half. "I'll let you know what's going on."

He didn't hug her before he left. Feeling exposed, Hannah retreated into the house.

At work Tuesday morning, Hannah kept it vague why she'd been out yesterday, but Dr. Pauline Griffin kept asking if everything was all right. Hannah should just have said she'd spent Sunday night vomiting because for some reason, "family crisis" invited far more curiosity than "crippling stomach bug."

Mid-morning, she got a call from Cashman at the computer repair shop. "I hate to be that guy, but after everything that happened last week, I was wondering if you could advise me with your veterinary expertise."

Hannah said, "Sure. What's going on with your cat?"

"He's not really my cat, but he's acting weird. He keeps positioning himself in front of me and looking up like he's asking for something. I think he's in pain. Ordinarily he despises me, and he makes a point of letting everyone else touch him even though I'm not allowed. But right now, it looks almost like I could pick him up. Is he sick?"

As if she could diagnose a cat over the phone. As if she could diagnose a cat at all. "I'd need to see him. Can you bring him in?"

"I guess. How would I do that?"

Of course. It wasn't his cat, so he wouldn't have a cat carrier. "Why don't I come get him? I also need to get my brother a new phone because everything went haywire on Friday."

Back in his lane, Cashman's tone changed from tentative to confident. "Technology haywire, or family dysfunction haywire?"

Hannah sighed. "My electronics are all fine."

"Unfortunately, I'm not a good tech for the other kind of haywire. My go-to at this point would be to take legal suggestions from your local constabulary."

It sounded like he was smirking, and she laughed despite herself.

Cashman added, "Mere common sense. They're familiar with the state statutes and how to apply them."

Hannah sighed. "The local constabulary, as you put it, got bored on Friday and involved themselves."

"Oh, bad move. They shouldn't have done that unless they could take the perp away in handcuffs."

"Friday night did end with handcuffs, and Monday night ended with my stuff in boxes in someone else's house. Oh, and I got custody of my younger brother. There may be spyware on his phone as well."

"That I can handle." Cashman paused. "The most dangerous time is when you get away from a control freak, so have you considered that there might be other tracking devices?"

Hannah found herself paraphrasing Susan. "There's nothing I can do about that, so I'm not going to worry."

Cashman said, "It turns out they make a scanner you can use to detect those, and it also turns out I have one on the desk right here."

That was...odd. And rather coincidental. "Sure. You can

scan my car and sell me a phone while I put your cat in a carrier and diagnose whatever's making him sick."

Abruptly Cashman was back to sounding uneasy. "I feel silly about the cat. I mean, it's probably nothing."

"Do you remember what I said when I brought you my phone?"

"That it was probably nothing? I don't actually remember," Cashman admitted. "Sure, let's do this."

Hannah went out to the front. "One of our clients asked me to pick up his cat because the cat seems to be having a crisis, only he doesn't have a carrier. I'll be back in fifteen minutes."

Dr. Griffin looked up, puzzled. "Which client?"

"The phone repair guy you recommended. The one who set up our network."

Her brow furrowed. "He doesn't own a cat."

"He does now." Hannah grabbed a spare carrier and three towels on her way out the door.

At the computer place, Cashman was on his knees, and with his arm fully stretched out, he was using just his fingertips to stroke the cat's head. The cat looked offended, but he wasn't leaving.

Sure, this wasn't Cashman's cat. "He's letting you touch him just fine."

"This is the first time. Something's up." Cashman stood, then winced. "How are you getting him into that cage?"

"Trust my skill set." She set a phone on the counter. "As for your skill set, this is the possibly-infected phone."

Cashman glanced at the phone. "That one's easy. I pick up cheap phones on eBay to refurb and resell, and I have its exact twin."

She'd been dreading in case Parker hated the replacement, so this was a relief. "Then I'll get the cat boxed up while you go all super-spy and sweep my car for a tracker."

Hannah very nearly toweled the cat, but the cat seemed so docile she decided just to pick him up. One scruff of the neck, and the cat went right in the box with the door locked behind him. He huddled inside, looking tiny.

Cashman withdrew. "Okay. Well." He seemed uneasy. "Ah, yeah, let me get my super-secret spy-sniffing device."

While Hannah tucked the carrier on the floor of the back seat, Cashman circled her car with a device the size of a pencil. Its red light flashed the whole way around the car. He felt the inside of the wheel wells and then searched around the tailpipe, although he did seem to be really cautious about standing again every time. "Lots of trackers are magnetic, and some of them don't broadcast. Those would need to be retrieved manually and then the data downloaded, which means they have to be quick to grab." He had her open the trunk so he could search the spare tire well. "Also, a lot of them don't track unless they're moving, that way they can save battery power. You'll want to use this while the car's in motion. If that light turns green, you've got a transmitter." Cashman checked under her dashboard and groped beneath the seats. "All the obvious places are clear. You can get the wand back to me later."

She said, "Sure, when you come for your cat. I'll call as soon as I know anything so you won't worry."

"I'm not worried." Cashman shrugged, but the motion was stiff and he wouldn't meet her eyes. "He's not really my cat. He just comes here."

Yes, yes, yes. Not really his cat. "*Some* people would be worried, so calling soon is our best-practices. By the way, where does the cat stay when it's cold? That wooden crate filled with straw and covered with a blanket?"

Cashman raised his eyebrows. "Go. Test out your car, and then tell me what's wrong with the cat who owns himself."

The light stayed red all the way back to the clinic, so that was a relief. Hannah ought to borrow the thing overnight, in case Tyler had slipped some kind of GPS in her belongings.

Before getting out of the car, she texted Enrique. "I'm in a spy movie. I have a tracker-sniffing device."

She checked in the cat with whatever information she knew. Cashman Lavera for the owner's name. She had his business phone number. Pet insurance? No. Pet's name?

She typed, "Not Really My Cat" because she couldn't remember if he'd told it to her. Given his general irreverence, he'd probably find it funny.

Enrique had texted her back. "Nice! I didn't know they made tracker-sniffing devices."

She replied, "Next I need a pen that blows tranquilizer darts and doubles as a safe-cracker."

"When we get a chance," she told Dr. Griffin, and it was a slow day, so they had a chance within half an hour.

Dr. Griffin sedated the cat in the carrier before taking him out. This was moderately dangerous given that they didn't know what was going on with the cat's system, but also a requirement with a cat that had no vaccines and no history of interacting with humans. Cashman said it had never bitten or scratched anyone, only rewarded them with lavish dirty looks and a lashing tail, but he'd been careful not to get too close.

Weight was good, although the cat was on the small side. Slight fever. Nothing felt broken. "I hope we're not dealing with poison." Then Dr. Griffin opened the cat's mouth. "Ah. There's our culprit, Watson. Call the owner so we can talk."

Hannah said, "There is no owner. It's not really Cashman's cat."

Dr. Griffin laughed. Sure, it wasn't his cat.

This was technically Hannah's lunch break, although the reality was that she got tiny breaks throughout the day and worked through the noontime hour while they fitted in extra patients or caught up from a surgery that took longer than anticipated. She called while walking through the parking lot onto the road leading away from Main Street. Hannah had taken her backpack, keeping the scanner in her other hand. It stayed red.

Cashman answered on the first ring. "Hey, Hannah. How is he? Did you figure it out?"

Yeah, he wasn't worried about that cat. Not one teensie bit.

Hannah said, "You were right that he was sick. He's got an abscessed tooth, and the infection traveled all along the side of the jaw. Treatment is surgically removing the broken tooth, and we can do that right away if you want."

"Do they recover from that? Will he still be able to hunt?"

Hannah stretched. The weather was nice today. "He'll be fine after a few days. This isn't uncommon."

Cashman sounded mystified but relieved. "Okay. That's good."

Hannah got her head out of the clouds and back into her job. "He'll need a week to recover from the infection and complete the course of antibiotics, so you'll want to keep him indoors."

Cashman's tone went lower. "I'm sunk, aren't I? After you took the cat, my wife had a huge laugh at my expense. She bet me five bucks she'd be buying a litter box and cat food on the way home tonight."

Hannah grinned. "What's your cat's name?"

Cashman sounded defeated. "I told you he's not really my cat."

Time to close the deal. "You knew him well enough to detect when he was in pain. You called me to make sure he'd be all right. Moreover, when the cat needed help, he trusted *you* to help him." Hannah paused just long enough to let that sink in. A musical score would call that a "fermata." "You can tell me all day long he's not really your cat, but as far as the cat is concerned, he thinks he's your cat."

Now Cashman sounded even more defeated. "His name is Braddy."

"He's in the database as Not Really My Cat, so I'll update that." Cashman didn't even chuckle. Hannah walked beneath maple branches that used to hang heavy with leaves. "We estimate he's five or six years old. How long have you had him?"

Cashman muttered, "About thirty seconds," and Hannah snorted a laugh. "I don't remember how long he's been hanging around. Maybe four years?"

"While he's under, we'd like to give him a rabies shot."

"A responsible owner would say yes, so fine."

"Also, should we neuter him? An intact male cat in a house isn't a great idea."

"If I'm going to have you chop off so many bits of him, I should have gotten a smaller cat. Fine, he hates me anyway." Cashman's voice pitched up. "Actually, I live out in the willie-wacks. I get coyotes. Moving him may be his death sentence."

"After a week, he'll be okay to go back to his regular life near your shop." She considered Cashman's particular speech patterns, then added, "Still, you may be surprised at how quickly he embraces the benefits of residing in climate-controlled luxury where food appears on a regular basis."

Cashman grumbled, "You're making fun of me."

"I totally am. Congratulations on your new cat."

Cashman sighed.

When she got off the phone, she remembered she hadn't told him about the tracker wand, but she'd be seeing him later anyhow.

A text had come in from Enrique. "How about an automobile invisibility cloak? That would be handy."

"Sure, until the first time I stop at an intersection and someone tries to drive through me." She wracked her brain for other devices. "I could use a robot dog."

For that matter, she could use a real dog. Parker had wanted Enrique to get between her and Tyler if it came to a fight, but Hannah had worked with more than one dog who would gaze upon you with adoring eyes—and would without a second thought rip out the throat of anyone who considered doing you harm. What if she could get a retired police dog? And what that would do to her chances of leasing an apartment?

An hour before they closed, Cashman showed up to

claim the—well, *his*—cat. Now that she could see him walking, he was clearly favoring one side.

Hannah leaned across the desk. "Are you hurt?"

He shrugged. "My wife and I ran a marathon on Sunday, and I'm still sore."

Hannah brightened "That's awesome! Did you win?"

He looked at her as if unsure how to reply. Then, "No."

She pulled up the file. "Oh, I'm sorry. How far was the race?"

He shrugged. "It's about an hour's drive north."

"I mean, how far did you run?"

Vaguely irritated, he said, "A marathon is always twenty-six-point-two miles. There's a really interesting reason for that, but if I start explaining, you'll save a lot of money on anesthesia." As she was about to hand him a printout, he raised his hands. "Please don't tell me what this cost. We're going to assume I have enough credit to pay for everything, and I will sign the receipt without looking."

Hannah shook her head. "It's not so bad. I'm charging for the neuter as if you're a rescue organization."

He looked up sharply. "Don't get in trouble. Whatever the difference in price, it's not worth your job."

That was a shock. Usually people pulled out the stops to pay less. "Dr. Griffin instructed me to charge that way because at the time, it wasn't your cat. Plus, you're about to owe your wife five dollars." Hannah handed him a plastic bag with two pill bottles and some squishy treats. "Braddy's going to need pain meds for a couple of days, and antibiotics for a week. Wrap the pill in the treat as if it's dough, and the cat should eat it. Canned food for the first few days until his mouth is healed. Nothing tonight." She paused. "Wait, are you from the running club? The one with the crazy wedding last summer?"

He nodded, then brightened. "Oh! You're from Aileen's cousin's string quartet. I have a friend who may give you a call next year, depending on whether his intended is surprised by his question or he's surprised by her answer."

Hannah laughed. "That's the kind of thing you should be

sure about before asking."

"Yeah, what idiot would propose on the spur of the moment? A special idiot might even do it twice." Smirking at a reference Hannah didn't get, Cashman signed the payment screen. "This is a terrible trade. I helped you scan for GPS trackers, and you gave me a cat."

He didn't look as irritated as he sounded. Hannah said reassuringly, "Most of our clients acquire their cats the same way."

Cashman frowned. "There's got to be a better system. Can I borrow your carrier to take him home?"

Was that the sound of an opportunity? Yes, it was. "Only if I can borrow your tracker to scan all my worldly belongings."

He perked up. "I wasn't planning to scan the cat tonight, so that sounds like a deal."

Hannah brought Braddy from the back, limp and loopy in his carrier. "He's topped up on pain meds and antibiotics, so start the pills tomorrow when he's hungry and won't be too picky."

"Exhausted, hungry, and in pain. I can relate." Cashman took the carrier. "Thanks for looking out for him. I certainly had no idea what I was doing. In fact, I still don't, but the cat survived in a parking lot for four years, so he'll probably manage in my living room."

Looking out for the cat was literally Hannah's job. Still, she watched through the window as Cashman set the carrier on the front seat of his car. Pause. Head cocked, he thought about it a few seconds. Then, still favoring one side, he reached back in to thread the seatbelt through the carrier's handle.

He was going to do just fine.

She texted Enrique. "I just matchmade a cat with an owner."

Enrique replied right away. "Do you do that often?"

She thought for a moment. Then, "I'm not a matchmaker, no. It's tricky to tell when things will work together."

Enrique replied, "But you harmonize great in the quartet."

That was an odd jump. "Are relationships like making music?"

From Enrique: "Exactly like making music. One goal, each of you taking a part, and the dynamics have to be right for each line to blend into the whole."

And again from Enrique: "When the parts are working together, there's nothing the music can't accomplish."

Hannah replied, "I like that."

Enrique sent, "I do too. It's what drew me to music in the first place."

Chapter Eleven

At age five, Enrique got his first tip for singing at a restaurant table.

He wasn't supposed to. He wasn't even supposed to be in the dining area, but the dining area was far safer than the kitchen with the knives and the burners and the hot water. From Day One of his life, he knew you don't play where everyone's working fast and everything's sharp and hot. If he didn't get killed when a line cook tripped over him, he'd get killed by his mother when she caught him in there.

Mom and Dad's restaurant took up all their time. Enrique had daycare, and he had his grandmother, but sometimes he had to come to the restaurant because no one else could take care of him. This one day, Enrique slipped out of Mom's office where he should have been staying with his teenage uncle, and he crept into the dining room.

The waitstaff were in a huddle near the kitchen. What was that for? Then someone lit a candle in a ball of deep-fried ice cream, and they paraded to a table to sing a happy birthday song. It wasn't the one Enrique knew from daycare, but he grinned because it was so much fun with all the waiters clapping, and they were such bad singers. After the waitstaff cheered, everyone laughed. The diner blew out his candle, and the waitstaff returned to their tables.

Enrique recreated the song in his head. The words didn't pair with the tune, but he worked them backward and forward. Changing a few words made them sound so much better, and then he changed the tune as well because it went better that way.

When no one was looking, he sprinted to where the guest was having his birthday party. Enrique stood at the end of the table with a big smile. "Happy birthday!"

The man with the ice cream smiled back. "Thank you! Are you lost?"

"No, sir!" Then Enrique sang the birthday song again, the better version that he'd fixed up. All four adults at the table applauded, and Enrique bowed the way singers bow on a cartoon.

His uncle swept over to him. "I'm so sorry! Enrique, you shouldn't be out here!"

His uncle was ten years younger than Dad, and Dad had a lot to say about his brother's sense of responsibility. Enrique wasn't supposed to have heard that either, but it was easy to slip around unnoticed when everyone was always busy.

The man with the birthday said, "He was wonderful! Great job!" and he gave Enrique a dollar.

A dollar? That was so cool.

After that, it would have taken chains to keep Enrique from getting out of the office. One of his favorite cartoons had a ton of songs. Enrique would hide until he found his mark, and once a path cleared to the table, he'd dart over to them and sing. Then he'd hold out his hand.

He was five. Any adult would give him a quarter just because he asked.

Eventually Mom gave up. As long as Enrique stayed out of the way of the servers, and as long as he asked first, he could pick one table every ten minutes and sing there. Grandma gave Enrique a watch and taught him to tell time. He trained himself to judge which people would give him a quarter so he didn't waste his chances. He got lots of quarters by the time he turned six, and he gave them to Grandma so now he was helping take care of the family.

One day, Mom sat with Enrique on the couch. "Would you like to sing more often than every ten minutes?"

He'd finished first grade, and it was summer vacation—the busiest season for the restaurant. Did he want to sing more? Sure! Mom gave Enrique a new set of rules, and now he was allowed to go through the restaurant at the top of every hour and ask each table if they wanted a song.

Years later, Enrique learned that during his "every ten minutes" phase, he'd sung for a restaurant critic. The critic found it off-putting and more than a little strange to be serenaded by the owner's kid and then shaken down for a quarter. The day after the review appeared ("Good food, but the singing kid needs to go") the waitstaff received a constant stream of tourists asking if Enrique would sing at their table.

Toward the end of the summer, a local family asked for a song. His classmate Lindsey Castleton was at the table, so Enrique backed away.

"I really want a song," said Lindsey's dad. "I heard that's why your restaurant is special."

With constant glances at Lindsey, Enrique picked a short song, then finished it fast. He wasn't even going to wait for his quarter.

"Don't go," said Lindsey's mom. "Can you sing this?" and did a series of ascending notes.

Cheeks hot, Enrique repeated them.

Mrs. Castleton said, "Now, do it again, but I want you to sing the note you think comes next."

Enrique started to back away, but then Mr. Castleton set a five dollar bill on the table.

Enrique's eyes went huge. Mr. Castleton said, "If you make my wife happy, this is yours."

What Mrs. Castleton wanted was really easy, so Enrique did it. Then she said, "Can you make it low like this?" and he did that too. Then she said, "Can you do all those notes backward?"

Singing backward was harder, but after he tried twice, he got it right.

Mrs. Castleton said, "Now, do that same progression while I sing a different set of notes."

That? Was super difficult. But it was also crazy fun, and it sounded terrific. Enrique laughed. "Can we do that again?" And then they did.

Mrs. Castleton said, "Now, I want you to sing the words, 'Magician, Musician,' and we'll keep singing them higher and faster."

That was funny and silly. Lindsey and Sierra sang it too, and by the end, their little brother was shrieking with laughter.

Enrique's dad came over. "Is everything okay?"

Enrique pointed to the table. "He's going to give me five bucks!"

Mrs. Castleton handed Dad her business card. "We own the music school on Granite Cross Road. Your son has an incredible talent and quite possibly perfect pitch. Once school starts up again and you don't need him in the restaurant every day, he'd really benefit from voice lessons."

Dad looked hesitant. Lindsey's father explained that Enrique would be able to do a lot more if he got the right training, and soon Enrique's Mom had joined them too. "At least let him do the first month for free," Mr. Castleton said. "If you don't hear a difference by then, I'll be shocked."

That September, Enrique took the school bus to the music school every Wednesday afternoon. Bob Castleton hired a voice coach just for him that one day a week, and the lessons were hard—but fun. Enrique practiced at home. He practiced in the lunch room. He practiced in bed at night when he was supposed to be asleep but Mom and Dad weren't back yet (and his irresponsible uncle was playing video games).

For years, it was all about voice. School chorus. Church choir. Community theater. After age eight, no one was interested in having a kid sing at their table, but that was when the Castleton Music School started hosting summer camps. Enrique learned to accompany himself on the piano. He learned guitar. His friends were all the other orchestra dorks, and at their cafeteria table they'd make jokes no one else would get. After school they'd head off to their chamber ensembles or drama productions (Hartwell was one of the few districts doing musicals) while the rest of the students scattered to do sports.

Enrique became comfortable with them all. Lindsey. Sierra. Hannah. Ashlyn. They ran in the same circles and had the same bizarre interests. An orchestra member would come to school lugging a leather case and open it in the cafeteria before the bell rang. "I found this at the secondhand shop. Any idea what it was?" The $1 tag would still be on the case, and Hannah would exclaim, "I think that's a cister!" and Lindsey would say, "No, it's a kamanche." The thing would be too wrecked to play, but they'd try to play it anyhow. Then the bell would ring and they'd scramble to wedge the thing back in the case, the mystery unsolved for now.

Music was Enrique's refuge. It was the thing that made him strange to his family but familiar to his friends. Music gave him a focus and an expertise. He joined a couple of garage bands and survived their breakups. He spent a summer with a theater group. He enrolled in music competitions alongside other Castleton students. He picked up paid gigs as a vocalist when his church needed a singer for weddings or funerals. He always returned to the Castleton Music School and the community of students.

Then came a scholarship from a national arts foundation, and Enrique would be the first person in his family to go to college.

The expectations: astounding. The uncertainty from his parents, the naked pride in his grandmother's eyes, the irritation from his brother—but overall, the hard, hard pressure to become the most successful singer the world had ever seen. He chose a state university and waited tables all summer (not singing) to afford a beater car and the occasional study night pizza. He worked off-campus jobs every semester and graduated magna cum laude with a dual degree in music and education.

Bob and Susan Castleton met him right after graduation, delighted to hug him and congratulate him, quick to offer him a chance to teach students at the music school, equally quick to recommend him as a vocalist for any function that needed one. The Hartwell school district hired him as a chorus teacher, and Enrique was all set. He'd escaped the family business. He was earning a living through music.

Many of his music friends moved out of town or entirely left Maine. Some weren't still in music, but the Castletons were. Ashlyn was, although she was an honorary Castleton. And Hannah, too—although until this year, Enrique hadn't seen much of her.

When he did, though, everything harmonized just the right way, and they made each other sound better than either one sounded alone.

The high school choir was excited beyond belief, and Enrique couldn't settle them until he forced them to do warmups. Something about the controlled breathing (not to mention making them sing far too loud and as high as they could go) always burned off the worst of the wiggles and giggles. Still, today felt like one of those days that would have had his sister-in-law checking if Mercury were in retrograde.

It would be nice to blame the heavens, but this most likely had nothing to do with anything outside Hartwell, Maine.

After warming them up, Enrique tried again to teach. "If you guys remember the volunteer hours conversation, I have good news! A number of places responded positively, so I'm setting up an after-school travel choir."

One of the kids shot up her hand, asking at the same time, "Where and how often because I also have to do basketball."

"Excellent questions, and ones I planned to answer in," Enrique checked the clock, "the next sentence. We'll practice two afternoons a week after school, and maybe one or two off-site performances on the weekend. So far, the skilled nursing facility is a definite, and the children's home would like us to visit at the same time as the gift drop-off. I've got feelers out with a half dozen other places, but between the rehearsal and performance hours, we should be able to get you guys significantly closer to the numbers you'll need for NHS or Scouts."

One of the girls raised her hand. Enrique said, "We'd try to keep to holiday-themed songs and be finished up by winter break."

The girl lowered her hand. Enrique said, "Would anyone else like to anticipate my next sentence?"

Giggles. One girl raised her hand. Enrique said, "We will use our holiday concert songs, but also mix in a number of popular standards to fill out the time we're there."

Her hand went down, then back up again. "Actually, I also wanted to ask if we were going to be performing *a capella*."

Enrique pointed at her. "That's a question I don't yet have an answer to. I would love to have accompaniment, but because we'll be working around the other organizations' schedules, there's no way to guarantee we'll always have musicians. If any of you or your friends volunteer to play guitar or keyboard, I'd be delighted, but we'll be prepared for anything. These won't be easy hours, but as with most volunteer work, you'll find they're worth all your effort."

One of the girls muttered, "Unlike my useless boyfriend."

Enrique said, "One assumes you didn't date your boyfriend for the service hours?" and the class laughed. "To keep this on task, I'm sending around a clipboard. If you want to volunteer, write your name. If you aren't sure, put your name in the second column so I know not to expect you. If you are sure you *don't* want to do it, don't bother writing your name at all. Your continued academic achievements are not in any way contingent on volunteering to perform."

One of the students raised her hand, and Enrique predicted the question. "That means I won't dock anyone's grade."

The hand went down. He was getting better at this.

"We'll meet after school Thursday in this room. Now, let's get back to Mozart."

The girl's offhand comment about her useless boyfriend grated on Enrique. Dating someone because they were useful wasn't a recipe for success. How would anyone like to hear that? "Of course I'd love to go to the prom with you! You have a car. What was your name again?"

He hoped Hannah didn't consider him useful. Granted, Hannah also didn't consider him her boyfriend. He'd made himself useful, but you do that for people you love.

Well—people you *like*. People you're friends with. Lindsey was hauling boxes for Hannah too, and Lindsey wasn't in love with Hannah. Same for Susan.

From a steely-eyed accountant point of view, Enrique had put far more into the nascent relationship than Hannah had. Why? Because right now Hannah was the one in need. He hadn't had feelings for her until he'd felt protective of her in the car, after which he'd just continued feeling...well, more. But especially protective.

Protecting the things you value was a natural extension of valuing them. Enrique found things his students left behind on a daily basis, leading him to believe they valued none of their personal belongings. It was a rare student who returned to ask if he'd left his hoodie. Usually for that to happen, it had to be raining.

If Hannah wasn't putting anything in right now, maybe she had nothing to put. Or maybe she didn't want to put anything in and Enrique was wasting both their times.

Still, though, when he remembered holding her on the couch, feeling her tension melt into his arms and her head slacken against his shoulder, he couldn't help but think she wanted something to be happening.

It didn't matter. Right now, he had to concentrate on high school students and Mozart.

CHAPTER TWELVE

Things to do this week:
   1) Find an apartment
   2) Move into the apartment
   3) Go to quartet practice. Twice.
   4) Raise Parker
   5) Prep for two performances over the weekend
   6) Have dinner with Enrique

One of Enrique's more attractive features to Hannah was how he had his life under control. She figured he knew what to expect when he woke up in the morning, and that gave him an assurance about expecting things for Hannah as well. He expected things to work out.

In her worst moments, Hannah struggled to trust that Enrique knew what he was talking about. All through high school, Enrique had been the dependable one. If someone hadn't done their homework and needed to scribble something into all the spaces on their math sheet, they'd ask Enrique and he'd hand it over. When the school had an awards ceremony, you'd hear "Enrique Almendarez" often enough that you could spell it backward. He showed up when he said he would. If Lindsey asked him to hang out after school, he'd ask his parents if he could do it.

Enrique saw a way forward, whereas Hannah felt unmoored. She used to talk to her mother every day. Definitely at the end of the day, but usually a couple of times during. She missed Mom. She missed her little brothers too. She missed having Bentley and Carter come into her apartment after dinner so she could read to them. She missed putting them to bed. She missed having her mother ask if she was chilly, if she'd eaten enough, if Dr. Griffin treated her well at the job.

Mom would have laughed about how Cashman acquired his cat. She'd have thought all the weird spy devices Enrique was joking about were funny, but by the same token, she'd have been worried by Enrique.

"You'll fall in love and leave me," Mom would have said, and Hannah would have reassured her that was silly. Enrique hadn't even kissed her. Meeting for dinner wasn't a betrothal.

Instead of Hannah's mother asking how Hannah was, there was Parker's social worker asking how Parker was. "He's getting along really well with Mrs. Castleton," Hannah said. She hadn't had time to call Caroline until she was driving home, and now she used the speakerphone. "They worked out the ground rules last night, and Mrs. Castleton texted me this morning with a list of things they agreed to. If I approve, she and he are both going to sign it as if it's a contract. It's things like she promises not to take away his phone as a punishment, and he promises to help clean the kitchen after dinner. He promises to do his own laundry, and she promises not to go through his stuff."

"Susan's got a good intuition for that." Caroline sounded pleased. "I've worked with her on some tricky cases. Her sixth sense tells her just how much space a kid needs, or sometimes how much structure."

"Well, Parker came home after school and checked in. They negotiated for thirty minutes, and then he went out with his friends. He can go hang out, but he has to get his homework done."

"I may have to intervene with that one, actually. I don't want him complicating things by getting in trouble, and groups of teenage boys tend to egg each other on. Parker has to stay away from the family home."

"He doesn't sound like he even wants to go back." Hannah flinched, thinking about the move-out supervised by cops. Mom hadn't left the bedroom to say goodbye.

Caroline said, "Do you have leads on an apartment?"

"Maybe?"

"Also, about Parker—given the seriousness of the charges against him...when we met with the DA and the judge today, we were able to get the charges downgraded, but he's going to have to do community service."

Hannah drawled out, "Okay... What kind? You're never going to get him to pick up trash from the side of the road." The traffic wasn't bad for October. She'd be home in fifteen minutes. "Susan got him to agree to clean the kitchen, but he sees that as part of letting us stay. He doesn't think it's fair he should be punished because Tyler went off the deep end."

"The judge doesn't see it that way. Parker went off the deep end too, and while it's terrific that he limited his violence to a car, it's better to get this nipped in the bud. Also, we're setting him up sessions with a therapist."

Hannah choked. "Good luck with that."

"Those are a condition of him remaining where he is rather than getting transferred to a boarding facility."

Hannah said, "Can I go in with him to the therapist?"

"We recommend family therapy in most cases, so yes, but we'll set that up with a different counselor."

Parker was going to blow his stack. For one thing, both Mom and Tyler had said since forever that psychiatrists only went into the field because they were crazy and wanted to fix themselves.

On the other hand, maybe Hannah could leverage Tyler's hatred of therapy to get Parker in the door. Parker would love to aggravate Mom and Tyler while seeming like the reasonable one. Just because he went to therapy didn't mean he had to reveal much. Hannah had gotten good at telling people what they thought they ought to hear without saying anything at all. Parker could develop the same skill.

Hannah said, "What about Mom and Tyler?"

"They have their own slate of things to do before we would attempt a reunion. I will require supervised visits to start, but right now they aren't indicating they want to see him."

Hannah said, "What if they try to see me?"

Even as she was saying it, a cold dread shot through her from head to foot.

Caroline said, "Tyler can't see you due to the restraining order. Do you want to see your mother?"

Hannah said, "I should. Right?"

Her mother had spent twenty years saying Hannah was "all I have." Then, when "all I have" was being threatened, her mother had found it possible to have something else.

Caroline said, "Why should you? I wouldn't. In fact, I would strongly recommend *against* seeing your mother."

That burn in Hannah's throat was guilt. She was supposed to be her mother's world. All along, she had been the good kid, never any trouble, always reliable, never too loud, always there to share her mother's interests and her mother's hopes and her mother's grief. Her mother would come home from a date and tell Hannah all about it before putting her to bed, and then in the morning, her mother would be daydreamy over coffee and tell her about it again. Hannah had been her mother's confidante all those years, and her mother had said, "Someday you'll leave me for a man."

Then in a moment, Mom had let Hannah go for a man.

Caroline said, "If your mother comes to you, at Susan's or at your apartment, you don't have to let her in. Because you're Parker's guardian, you have a say over who he sees. Even if she demands because she's his mother, it's your call."

Mom would badger her. Mom would layer on the guilt. Mom would cry because two of her children had allied against her. It wouldn't be the first time.

Hannah said, "When can Parker and I get in to see the family therapist? We need to come up with guidelines, and I need to know what Parker wants in case we're ever in that situation."

"That's a good point. Tomorrow night we could meet in my office and work that out ourselves."

Tomorrow night Hannah was supposed to be seeing Enrique for dinner. Enrique wouldn't mind if she cancelled. He'd been straightforward about what her priorities should be.

It was just...she didn't want to. Blast it, she'd given up so much so many times for other people's obligations. Everyone else made their own lives easier at Hannah's expense, over and over, every time.

Once, just once, she wanted to do something for herself that made her feel good.

Caroline said, "What time do you get back in town? Please say it's before five."

"It's always after five. I could go in late, though, if we could meet early in the morning."

Caroline said, "Thank you. That would be so much better."

They set up an appointment for Thursday morning. She'd keep Parker out of school.

She'd see Enrique for dinner.

She'd see Enrique for dinner, and it surprised her how much she was looking forward to that.

CHAPTER THIRTEEN

Enrique looked great leaning against a pillar outside Paolo Lui's, Hartwell's Italian restaurant. They both smiled and then kept an awkward distance as if neither of them knew what should happen. Hannah certainly didn't. Hug him? Shake hands? Perform a ceremonial dance?

Enrique said, "Right on time. Ready?" and held the door for her. Hannah went inside with her hair standing on end and her skin warm from how close he was.

This was definitely a date. Their lunch at the Hartwell Diner had been triage. Him moving her out of her house was a military action. The dinner at Susan's afterward was a debriefing.

This, just her and him, was a date.

Hannah had Googled everything last night, desperately glad her stepfather was no longer spying because she was searching things like, "What to talk about on a date" and "How to dress for a date." If it didn't involve stage makeup and concert blacks, Hannah had no idea how to make an outfit work.

Interesting question, and this was not one of Google's suggestions for what to talk about on a date: if someone installed spyware and then died of boredom, were you guilty of manslaughter?

Hannah stared at the menu. It wasn't fascinating reading. In between, she kept glancing up at Enrique.

He seemed puzzled. "You're nervous."

Of course she was nervous. This was a date. "Aren't you?"

Enrique shook his head. "I wanted to go out because I like being with you. Although now you're making me nervous."

Hannah's eyebrows shot up. "At least I have one skill set?"

"I think you have several. Tell me about matchmaking the cat."

She explained about swapping out Parker's phone, ("Good thinking," Enrique interjected,) followed by the rest of the cat's saga. "It's sweet and funny. Cashman and the cat bonded through mutual disdain, but somehow it turned into respect."

Enrique sat back. "I bet you witness a lot of horrible things at your job, so it's good to see something cute."

"This isn't the job for you if you're already cynical, yeah." She shuddered. "After three weeks working there, I started to dread the phrase 'former owner.' As in, former owner moved and didn't take the cat, or former owner surrendered the dog because it got too big."

Enrique's gaze darkened. "I hate that."

"I hate it too. The poor animals get abandoned. The lucky ones, that is. The unlucky ones—I've had to assist at pet autopsies in abuse cases." Hannah froze. "Oh. Sorry."

Pet autopsies weren't on the list of suggested topics for first dates. She should have stuck to the weather and Enrique's favorite desserts.

Enrique didn't look horrified. "Don't be sorry. It's your

job. How did you get into being a vet tech in the first place? It's a far cry from music."

"My mother said I needed a field that would make money, and playing music doesn't usually make enough to survive. In college, I was volunteering with an animal rescue group, and one summer I got to intern with a veterinary clinic. That convinced me it was a good fit if I couldn't make it as a cellist."

Enrique said, "And you do like it?"

She rested her chin on her hands. "I do. I love seeing the animals and how they interact with their people. They're all so different together, but the good owners are so protective. They're thinking for their pets, looking out for them, and they're not in it for themselves. Some of the cats are so scared, and some of the owners are so reassuring—but they're reassuring in so many different ways. Every so often you'll get an unusual animal like a chinchilla or a hedgehog, and those are fun."

There were the sad situations too. Her clinic held those appointments in the nicer room with the soft curtains and the print of a bridge constructed of rainbows. During those appointments, Hannah got to be the soft shoulder, the comforter, the voice of understanding. "You were there for her right to the end," she'd say. "You loved her, and she knew it. You were all she had in the world, so you took the very best care of her."

Again, not a thing to talk about on a first date. Hannah should have written a list. It was too late to go back to the website now, stumbling through sentences while looking at the phone. *"So, Enrique, um...tell me about your favorite summer vacation."*

Come to think of it, she'd probably lived through his favorite summer. Maybe one of those Castleton Music camps where they all prepared for the statewide competition at the end of August.

Time to admit defeat. "Okay, enough about my job. Tell me something I don't know about you."

One of the articles insisted that guys enjoyed talking

about themselves, so this was a good thing to ask.

Enrique thought. "By now, don't you know everything?"

"There's plenty I don't know." She considered a moment. "Um...where was the last vacation you went on?"

Enrique snickered. "My brother took me white-water kayaking because his wife wouldn't go with him."

Hannah laughed. "White-water kayaking?"

"*Competitive* white-water kayaking." Enrique rolled his eyes. "I made peace with the universe that I'd had a good run, but I was going to die."

Hannah imagined a lake full of two-man kayaks, each paddle tipped with spikes, each kayaker wearing an armored life vest. "I didn't know people did that."

"Neither did I until he picked up our numbers!" Enrique had Hannah laughing now, and warmth spread through her. "First it was just, 'Let's go kayaking.' Then it was, 'Oh, and it'll be Saturday and Sunday.' Sure, whatever. Then, 'Oh, and we have to be at the pier at seven o'clock in the morning.' So help me, he taught me on Saturday, and we were in the competition on Sunday."

Hannah raised her water glass. "And yet, you survived."

"I survived. I nearly pitched out of the kayak twice, and we were going so fast I was sure my mother would get a doorbell ring from the boys in blue." He made his face grim. "*Mrs. Almendarez, we regret to inform you that your sons are stupid.*"

Hannah prompted, "But it worked out?"

"Not at all. My brother didn't talk to me for the whole ride home and for three weeks after because I lost my paddle, and if you can imagine, it's a problem to have to do a two-man kayak solo."

Hannah's eyes widened.

Enrique glanced at the ceiling. "I wasn't sorry at all. He deserved it."

She snickered. "But was it fun?"

"Learning? Yes. Doing it on Saturday on flat water in a lake was a lot of fun, but I should have known something was up that Sharon didn't want to go with him." Enrique grinned. "Then he took me out onto the rough water, and that was kind of fun too, although I kept telling him I wasn't ready. The next day? That was all on him."

Hannah said, "I've never kayaked."

"I'll take you sometime." Enrique paused. "On flat water. In ten months, when it's not thirty degrees out."

Hannah said, "Thirty Celsius, maybe?"

"Oh, you just reminded me, I came home sunburnt like a lobster. That's the reason *I* wasn't talking to *him* for the ride home. Daniel hasn't invited me on any adventures since."

Their meals arrived. Hannah had a momentary panic remembering the girls in high school saying there was no way they could ever eat in front of a guy. It was ridiculous. She'd devoured one of those five-napkin burgers beside him a couple of weeks ago. For that matter, he'd asked her out right after they'd had dinner at Susan Castleton's home. He was under no delusion that she didn't eat anything in order to maintain her beautiful figure. (Neither part, actually).

Enrique said, "Now your turn. Tell me something about you that I don't know."

Wide-eyed, she burned with shame.

He was looking pleased and relaxed, and his easy smile meant he thought it the natural next step of the conversation. She'd asked because an expert suggested it in an article, and he'd asked because he wanted to know.

Still, she couldn't come up with something fun like competitive white-water kayaking and instead felt only her millions of inadequacies tumbling together like pieces of cereal sliding into a breakfast bowl. Something he didn't know about her? He didn't know what a disappointment she was, and he didn't know it because she never let anyone see unless they witnessed it by accident.

Unless he was testing her because he'd already seen it and wanted to know if she'd admit to it.

Instead she said, "Do you know I broke my arm when I was eight?"

"I vaguely remember that." Enrique thought. "I may have signed the cast."

Mom had worried about Hannah for months. Any time they went outside, Mom had to hover and make sure Hannah wouldn't get re-injured. She badgered the doctor to give her a note excusing her from gym and recess for the rest of the school year after the cast came off—just in case.

Hannah shrank into the seat. "This is a tough question because you may know everything about me."

Enrique said, "I would have said that too, but in the last two weeks, I've been surprised by how much I didn't know."

She lowered her eyes. "What hadn't you known?"

His voice softened. "How difficult you had it. You never talked about your family. You were very private, and I figured you wanted it that way."

She shuddered. "It's really unnerving how much everyone found out all at once. It's like getting stripped naked at the shopping mall."

Enrique looked sad. "I'm sorry I never paid attention to any of this before. I might have been able to see it."

"What would you have seen?" She met his eyes. "It was nothing huge. It still isn't for me. The thing with Parker is huge," she amended. "That, I don't know how to handle. I'm glad Susan's leading the way, but once we get an apartment, it's going to be just me and him. Although I do have a meeting with Caroline tomorrow."

For all that this conversation made Hannah uneasy, Enrique was having not one single problem eating his meal. She wondered briefly if he was paying for both of them, and if he'd be offended if some of her meal went home with her in a box. The articles didn't mention leftovers.

He said, "What gets decided tomorrow?"

"We need to talk about family therapy, and guidelines about my mother. Social work is going to ask Parker to do some kind of community service, too, and he's going to hate it."

Enrique brightened. "Send him to me!"

Hannah laughed. "You're a community service organization?"

He mock-bowed to her. "Indeed, my lady, I am. The high school has started a chamber group for the sole purpose of garnering community service hours by singing for worthy causes."

Hannah blinked at him. Parker. Singing. In an ensemble.

That would never happen.

Although... Parker had volunteered Enrique's apartment for them to live in, so he must find Enrique tolerable. "Tell me more."

It turned out Enrique had cobbled together the whole project on his own. "Music helps people. You know that." He was so passionate as he told her the story. Songs lifted people's spirits. Some people had nothing to look forward to at the holidays. Some kids had no happy memories of the holidays. Live music was a way to reach out to individuals who otherwise might feel lonely the whole time, and it was a concrete way to show they were valued.

Hannah said, "So you'll visit the same places every week? That way it doesn't look like a hit-and-run raid?"

Enrique paused. "Do you think we should?"

"If you're talking about people looking forward to something and feeling valued, yeah, a repeating event would be better than a one-off."

Enrique fell quiet, and Hannah wished she hadn't said anything beyond, "That sounds great!"

"That's a good point. I want people to feel served, not like the object of a service project." Enrique met her eyes. "All I meant is, Parker could join. He'd be with other high school students, and he'd pick up four hours a week on an ongoing basis."

Hannah opened her hands. "You don't have to convince me. I happen to believe in the power of music. He's going to think it's ridiculous, and he'll tell you he can't sing."

"Part of the fun is most of the other kids can't sing

either." Enrique smiled wryly. "I'm going to recruit outside the school chorus, and in a group like that, you don't have to be a coloratura soprano."

He gave a rundown of the places they'd already committed to sing at, and Hannah interrupted halfway through. "That's where Bob is."

Enrique stopped cold. "Oh. You're right."

"That's not a reason not to sing there."

"Yeah, I just—" He looked aside. "Blast. It's hard seeing what's happened to him."

"I hate it too. I don't think he remembers me anymore."

Frontotemporal dementia was not on the list of first date conversation topics, but by now Hannah had strayed so far from that list that there was no saving anything. They were just riding the conversation wherever it led, and Enrique was going to consider it a wasted date. Talking about life, death, love, loss, value, passion—that drilled so much deeper than, "What is your favorite movie?"

She looked down. "I'm sorry. I keep dragging us down. You could be having a great time, and instead it's all this heavy stuff."

Enrique sat back. "I thought we were both having a good time."

Hannah bit her lip. "I'm not being lighthearted and flirty."

Enrique sighed. "Thank heaven, because I'm not being dashing and suave."

Despite herself, Hannah giggled. "I've seen romance movies. Either there's supposed to be wacky hijinks, or else I'm supposed to be beautiful."

"I happen to think you are, and the last time I had wacky hijinks, my brother didn't talk to me for two weeks."

He reached across the table for her hand, and Hannah reached back.

"You've got a lot going on." He squeezed her hand, and she looked into his eyes. He was smiling. "You're telling me things about you that I didn't know."

Hannah shook her head. "I haven't told you anything."

"You just told me you think about how other people perceive things. You told me you care about making sure everyone is happy." He wove his fingers through hers. "You've told me you're nervous about being in the spotlight, and you're appreciative of the work others do. You never let me see your depth before."

Hannah didn't let go of his hand even though it was scary to be seen. "You're reading a lot into me."

"You're also not one to accept a compliment." Enrique let her go, but he didn't take his eyes from hers. "In lieu of that, maybe you'll accept dessert. After dinner, we can see about convincing Parker to join the chorus."

CHAPTER FOURTEEN

Cars filled the driveway and curb of the Castleton home when Enrique pulled up, making it look like a party when in actuality it was just Susan inviting her children and adjacent-children.

Ages ago, Susan had stifled a laugh when someone suggested having eight people for Thanksgiving was like cooking for an army. Enrique had been about to ask how many Susan cooked for on a regular basis when Susan sweetly offered that person an invitation to dinner one night, so they'd have a break.

"That's the way you do it," she told Enrique later. "Don't correct. Just show them."

Inside the house was noise, and the noise led to a farmhouse table in a kitchen crowded with people and littered with the remains of dessert. "Hey!" Lindsey exclaimed. "Guys, make room for them."

Chairs started shifting around the table. Enrique and

Hannah weren't facing an army, but maybe a platoon. Susan. The three Castleton kids: Lindsey, Sierra, and Corwin. The previously-unknown Castleton, Michael. The Castletons' almost-kid, Ashlyn. The new kid, Parker. And now the two of them.

Pink-cheeked, Hannah looked uncomfortable, so Enrique had her sit first. Susan got them a pair of mismatched plates and passed the remainder of the cake down the table.

Lindsey said to Corwin, "Okay, before you change the subject again: how exactly did you make an amplifier explode on stage?"

Corwin threw his hands in the air. "It wasn't my fault, okay!"

If Hannah hadn't been sitting ramrod straight, Enrique would have put his arm around her. This chaos felt familiar even though he'd only eaten in this house a few times. His own extended family gatherings were similar: food and humor, everyone trading stories that were simultaneously self-aggrandizing and marginally embarrassing. There would be the occasional fight and the not-so-occasional political discussion which would end up with everyone agreeing that everyone on all political sides was in it for themselves.

With Hannah so tense, he instead put his hand on her leg under the table. Then she tensed even more and looked at him in mild panic.

Ashlyn called down the table, "You have to try one of Michael's cookies!"

Michael protested, "Don't! I only brought them so you guys could laugh."

Corwin said, "They aren't so bad if you soak them in milk for five minutes," and Michael laughed just as hard as he did.

"I thought they were nice!" Frowning, Ashlyn turned to Enrique. "Michael never baked cookies before, but he wanted to make something to bring for dinner."

Susan said, "You didn't have to."

Lindsey leaned into, "You really didn't," and Sierra shot back, "Rude!"

Michael said, "We weren't exactly bakers growing up."

Susan sighed. "They're fine."

Parker said to Hannah, "You've made cookies."

"On snow days, when the littles needed something to do." Hannah averted her eyes. "It's fun."

Enrique shrugged. "Don't look at me. My parents are chefs, but I only learned to cook when I moved out of their house."

Michael grinned. "Necessity is an excellent teacher. Necessity and Google."

Lindsey called, "Hannah! Update as of two hours ago! The mom of one of my students has an apartment. I haven't seen it, but she says you can swing by tomorrow. It's right in town, and you'll have a parking spot."

Hannah nodded. "Maybe we can both look in the morning. Parker, Caroline wants to meet us at nine. I'm going into work late, and I'll call you in late to school."

Parker groaned. "Oh, just what I want. Instead of sitting bored in class, I can sit bored in an *office,* talking about my *feelings.*"

"Actually, there's something else." Hannah glanced at Enrique. "Don't get mad, but one of the things Caroline said was they want you doing some kind of community service."

Even Enrique, who had seen eye-rolls from a thousand high school students, was impressed by the rotation and degree of drama Parker managed to achieve with this one. "Ooh, do I get to pick up trash by the highway?"

Enrique said, "I have a better suggestion. I'm starting a volunteer choir where we'll sing at local nursing homes as community service through the holiday season. It'll be a lot more fun than picking up trash, and a whole lot warmer."

Parker stared at him. "Really?"

Corwin frowned. "Where will you be singing?"

Enrique said, "We'll be at the facility where your father

is staying."

Corwin nodded. "Let me know what day. I bet we can get a bunch of concerts going there if Dad wants."

Sierra looked sad. "Dad's weird about music. Sometimes he wants to hear it. Sometimes it just makes him upset."

Susan shook her head. "It's better to offer it than not. If you let me know what days, I'll make sure to be there. If he gets agitated, I'll take him out again."

Hannah leaned forward. "Parker, doing this would get you four hours a week. Two hours after school, and two hours performing on weekends. That'll keep social work off our backs and make the authorities look harder at what Tyler was doing."

Enrique said, "Let Tyler dig his hole deeper while you convince everyone you were never the problem to begin with."

Parker shook his head. "I get it. But seriously, this is dumb. Singing isn't community service."

Susan said, "On the contrary, singing creates community. Music creates stories and history and identity."

Parker rewarded her with another eye-roll, although only half as dramatic as the one he'd given Hannah. "Then when some judge gets my case, he's going to say, 'Did the kid build houses for the homeless? No, even better, the kid sang at a nursing home! Let's marvel at all the community he built!'"

Hannah said, "Caroline knows the judge, and she said community service is what will work best for you."

Parker folded his arms. "It's stupid. But everything about this situation is stupid, so sure."

Corwin left, followed shortly by Sierra. Ashlyn and Michael

walked out to his car, and Lindsey went into one of the back rooms with her mother to look for some sheet music. Parker dropped himself on the couch with his phone.

Enrique took Hannah's hand. "Come outside a minute."

On the porch, he rested his forearms on her shoulders. "Are you okay? You got so tense."

"They're noisy. Dinners at home... Even the little ones knew to stay quiet." She shuddered. "Everyone here was so loud and blustery."

Enrique chuckled. "In my family, if everyone's quiet during a big dinner, that's unnerving. It means we're all angry."

"Like I broke your kayak paddle?" She met his gaze. "They do everything different here. Even the way they talk. Susan doesn't talk down to Parker like he's a kid. Neither do you. Everyone's listening to him. He's got as much control as possible in a situation that's out of control."

Parker wasn't what Enrique wanted to be talking about. He fingered the hair at the base of Hannah's neck. "Different, but not bad."

"Everyone's being good to us." She didn't pull away from his touch. "Thank you for dinner."

He leaned in. "It wasn't awful, having a date?"

"It wasn't as bad as I was afraid it would be." Wow, endorsement of the century, right there. She looked away. "I didn't mean it like that. What I mean is I didn't mess everything up. Although I guess I'm messing it up now."

She was about to apologize. Instead, Enrique kissed her.

His lips met hers gently, and she went still. He didn't linger. Heaven knew he wanted to linger, to embrace her and keep her there. Yet if he did that, she'd recoil—and he didn't want her to retreat. Instead he kept it quick and soft and then stayed near because although he had the willpower not to push for more, he also didn't have quite enough to step away.

She smiled. Their faces were still so close. He could do it again if he tried.

She whispered, "Thank you."

"I had a good time tonight." He stroked the hair at the base of her neck. She was tantalizing. She didn't believe she was beautiful, and she didn't feel as if she had the right to be attractive to him. He should have seen it years ago. If he'd been closer to her for years, maybe now he could have pulled her against his chest and nuzzled her neck and kissed her boldly, and maybe she'd have been enthusiastic rather than skittish. "When can I see you again?"

Lost, Hannah said, "I don't know."

No, of course she didn't. Enrique said, "If you get an apartment, ping me. At the very least, I can haul boxes."

It was too practical a way to end the evening, but she was too unnerved to accept anything more.

Michael's car pulled away, and Ashlyn came up the walk. They had no time. Enrique said, "Can I have one more?"

Hannah giggled. "Yes."

He kissed her again, kissed her quick, kissed her knowing he had a long road to convince her he was for real.

CHAPTER FIFTEEN

Enrique had kissed her.

Far too late at night, Hannah lay in Lindsey's childhood bedroom staring at the ceiling and thinking about Enrique.

He'd kissed her twice. He might even have kissed her a third time, except that Ashlyn returned, and then Lindsey came out of the house. When Ashlyn stepped onto the porch, Enrique stepped back from Hannah and let go, and three hours later, she still felt that same combination of joy and let-down. She'd wake up tomorrow feeling it, then wander through the rest of the day wondering what to think about his sudden distance.

He'd ended the date with a kiss, which the articles suggested was a good thing.

He hadn't wanted to be seen kissing her. Which Hannah wasn't sure wasn't a bad thing.

True, she hadn't wanted to "get caught," as if a kiss were something shameful. What a kiss was—witnessed—was a commitment. She already felt weird and awkward that everyone knew he'd taken her on a date. If she and Enrique kept going on dates, even total strangers would glance at the two of them and assume they knew what she and Enrique felt.

For years, no one was supposed to know what she felt. Hide it. Bury it. Be quiet. Be no trouble at all. Be the reliable one. Be the one who understands.

When she and Enrique walked in, everyone's expectant looks had left Hannah feeling like Eve scrambling for the nearest fig leaf.

It was easiest to believe Enrique was merely nice, that he felt sorry for her and had taken her out to distract her from the tumult. She could tell herself he'd ended with a kiss (well, two kisses) because that's how a nice guy ends a date. When there were witnesses, though, he'd backed away. The question was whether he didn't want to get her in trouble, or whether he was ashamed of her.

The answer to that, Hannah supposed, was whether he wanted a second date. She'd have to wait and see. That was okay. People's future behavior was how they let you know what they'd meant all along.

On the other side of the wall, Parker was in Sierra's old bedroom. Hannah couldn't hear him moving around, but this mid-1800s farmhouse had solid walls, so she wouldn't be able to hear anything even if Parker were doing jumping jacks. While technically she was responsible for him, in reality Susan had been doing everything. Susan had been in charge tonight so Hannah could have her date. Susan had stepped right into the role of being a responsible adult without even once seeming as if she were mothering Parker.

Which, perhaps, she was also doing for Hannah.

Hannah had a mother, but here stood Susan enfolding Hannah right into the family chaos in a way not like a guest and not like a child. She'd taken over negotiations and decisions and even "childcare" (although Parker would have gagged if anyone called it that).

Susan couldn't save her own husband. Bob not living at home must mean Bob's needs exceeded her ability to care for him, and for a woman so capable—that helplessness must be like an acid dissolving her from the inside out. Instead, Hannah was someone she could save. But Hannah was supposed to be bolstering her own mother.

Eyes screwed shut, Hannah flipped over in bed and hated herself. Hated herself for being the object of Susan's effort when Susan's husband was dying. Hated herself for being in need when she was supposed to be the person who never caused anyone even a moment of trouble.

Hated herself in case Enrique really had been ashamed.

Hated herself in case she was falling for Enrique. She had too many other people relying on her. It wasn't right to think of herself. Not now. Not like this.

If Enrique really wanted to go out with her again, though, she might start falling for him after all. And she hated herself for that too.

Enrique looked puzzled. "The traditional moving dinner is pizza."

Hannah shook her head. "Pizza is expensive, and I haven't cooked in ten days."

Moving day. Hannah and Parker had an apartment.

Lindsey's student's mother's house had a third-floor unit with a mild draft, a tiny kitchen, two bedrooms wedged under the eaves, and a bathroom with a shower stall. Parker grumbled that they were going to freeze, but Hannah thought it more likely they'd get whiplash from the temperature extremes: drafts and goosebumps until the heat went on in the main house, after which they'd be sweating in short sleeves.

Didn't matter. The price was right. The location was

good. The apartment was available.

With nearly no furniture, the move went fast. Parker and Enrique maneuvered the futon up the narrow back staircase, and the rest of it was just boxes and trash bags. "We'll get it unpacked later," she insisted, but Enrique helped her at least unbox her kitchen stuff. When she found the dry goods, she said, "Hey, dinner!" Hannah dispatched Parker to the corner store to get a half gallon of milk and a block of cheddar cheese, and she started boiling water for pasta.

A knock on the door, and Hannah went cold inside. After one look at her face, Enrique answered the door instead.

It turned out to be Hannah's new landlady with a plate of cookies. "I just wanted to make sure everything was all right."

Enrique grinned like a fiend after the landlady left. "You know why people do that, right?"

Hannah set the cookies on the counter. Her landlady had provided dessert, and these had to be better than Michael's attempt. "To be nice? To welcome me as her tenant?"

Enrique snickered. "It's spying, but friendly-like."

Hannah's hair stood on end as she glanced at the cookies. "Should I have turned them down?"

"Of course not. It's a polite fiction. It's illegal for her to barge into the apartment and see what you're doing, but it's perfectly legal to give you cookies and then glance over your shoulder at what's going on." He gestured to the door. "Here's the problem we've just discovered, though. You don't have a peephole. If someone knocks, you can't tell who it is."

She shivered. "I never had that at home either."

At home. Not her home anymore.

Enrique shook his head. "Back then, you didn't have a restraining order against anyone."

"Speaking of that, I need to give back Cashman's GPS detector, except I packed it and don't know where."

Hannah shook her head. "Oh, and my mother told Caroline I had approved the spyware because I was afraid of wrecking my car during my commute. That way they could find me if my car plunged into the woods. Off 1A. You know, that unknown road no one travels."

Enrique's eyes widened. "Your mother expected anyone to believe that?"

"Supposedly she had no idea it would take pictures with my camera and log all my passwords, and she doesn't understand why it would have looked like Tyler was trying to access all my accounts a couple of days after I switched phones and changed everything, but all of them getting hacked then was a terrible coincidence."

Enrique rubbed his chin. "Wow. What really bad luck for Tyler."

Hannah rolled her eyes. "Also, I must be mistaken about seeing his IP address logged into my Gmail account, even though we have screenshots. Amazingly, Caroline wasn't born last Wednesday, so she noted my mother's explanation and went on with her life. The spyware doesn't even matter to them because it doesn't pertain to Parker's case, but my mother's excuse-making does."

The new apartment was more like a campout. Other than the futon and a couple of book shelves, they'd be living out of (and off of) boxes until she could cobble together money for furniture or find freebies. She'd bought a pair of air mattresses and a few other essentials. Parker had gotten back his clothes, but he hadn't even retrieved his toothbrush.

Parker returned with the cheese, so Hannah started a cheese sauce for the macaroni, and then she set the macaroni and cheese into the apartment's tiny oven. She'd need to do a real grocery trip tomorrow.

Watching alongside her at the counter, Enrique said, "I never made mac and cheese that wasn't from a mix."

"It's cheaper from the box, but not as good." Hannah sighed. "We'll probably revert to that because it's nice having a whole meal for two dollars, but tonight you get the real stuff."

Parker leaned against the wall, arms and ankles crossed. "Is that how it works? The guy takes the girl out to a restaurant, and in exchange she cooks him a meal for under ten bucks?"

Hannah bristled, but Enrique only shrugged. "I like home-cooked meals. Especially when I didn't have to cook them."

Parker screwed up his face. "The system isn't fair. If you have to take Hannah to a restaurant, she should have to take you to a restaurant."

Enrique raised his hands. "No one forced me to take her to a restaurant. I could have cooked for her instead."

Hannah said, "That would have been fine."

Enrique's eyes lit up. "Then how about you both come over tomorrow night?"

Parker pretended to be delighted. "Yeah, that's an awesome date! You and your girlfriend...and her little brother!"

Hannah wasn't sure what part of that sentence to correct first, but Enrique's eyes lit up. "My grandmother used to have to bring her brother on dates to 'chaperone,' so my grandfather used to pay him off to leave them alone."

Hannah laughed. "Really?"

Enrique was grinning. "Parker, my mother hereby requires you to chaperone me and Hannah. You can measure the distance between us with a ruler and report to her if I hold Hannah's hand. I'm sure that's exactly how you want to spend your evening."

Parker looked disgusted. "It's a toss-up between that and driving a railroad spike through my skull with a sledgehammer. I'm leaning toward the spike. If you want to pay me off, though...?"

Enrique laughed. "Come over at six. Both of you."

Tingles went up Hannah's spine. "It's a date?"

Enrique paused. "Well, yes—but if it's going to make you nervous, I'm just making dinner, and then we can watch something on TV."

Parker stalked out of the narrow kitchen. "You guys are making me sick." He slammed his bedroom door hard enough that the kitchen cabinet doors bounced.

Enrique stepped toward her and lowered his voice to a mockery of a radio announcer. "Alone at last." Hannah giggled.

He didn't quite stop. He put his hands on her waist and drew her closer. She laid her hands on his shoulders, then it felt even better to rest her cheek against his. He smelled of cologne and cardboard boxes, and his beard prickled against her skin.

Enrique murmured, "Would you like a second date?"

Hannah folded into him. "I would."

"Turn up tomorrow, and I'll cook for you." He hesitated. "Well, after my cooking, you might not want a third date."

Hannah smiled. "I'm making you macaroni and cheese. You're going to beat that without even trying."

"Mac and cheese is comfort food." He felt so strong against her. "It's nice just to share a meal with you."

It was the perfect moment, so naturally her phone buzzed. Enrique released her.

Hannah looked away, shy. "The phone could wait."

Enrique raised his hands. "Not when you have social workers and district attorneys breathing down your neck."

He had a point. She pulled her phone from her pocket, and her heart stopped.

For the first time in weeks, her mother had texted.

"Hannah, honey, your little brothers miss you so much. You need to stop this nonsense and come home for them."

CHAPTER SIXTEEN

Parker slunk into the after-school chamber music club looking by turns humiliated and furious. An excellent start.

A tally of Enrique's volunteer chorus gave him ten singers, two guys and eight girls—and neither guy was in the regular chorus. "For starters, I need to learn your names." Enrique paced the front of the room. "For those of you not taking chorus, you've probably figured it out, but I'm Mr. Almendarez, and you can call me Mr. A. Miranda, I know you." Miranda waved. "Can the rest of you please tell me who you are? And use your real names because it's embarrassing to have the front office paging Festus Swett."

Glowering in his seat, Parker didn't crack a smile, but the other kids offered many names, including Ima Genius and Ben Dover. Enrique gave a five-second rundown of the group project, during which another student entered, and one of the chorus kids shouted, "It's Ben's sister! Ilene

Dover!" Once again, no singing took place.

Enrique had loved choral chaos as a student. As a teacher, not so much.

Although Enrique didn't know which kids hung out with each other, he sensed that these weren't Parker's regular friends. Well, then: mix things up and get them talking. He expected to lose a couple of his volunteers, but Parker couldn't be one.

"First things first." Enrique handed out song lists. "Let me know if there's anything here you refuse to sing, or if there's anything left off that you feel compelled to sing. Everyone has a Christmas song they hate, and I've got no interest in forcing you to sing those." He raised his voice as everyone proposed songs so hateful they must never be sung again. "However, keep in mind that you get exactly one absolute veto. Anything after that is a suggestion, so choose carefully. If two of you veto the same song, neither of you gets a do-over."

There, that should get them talking.

Moments later, there was so much talking that Enrique couldn't hear his own thoughts.

Parker looked as if he'd just as soon veto every single song ever written. He had Hannah's eyes and smile, but the rest was so different. Where she was brunette, he was blond. Her storm-cloud eyes stood in contrast to his hazel ones. Their mannerisms, though, were similar. They did the same thing after they laughed, averting their gaze as if ashamed that you'd caught their moment of joy.

Nine years apart. Raising him was a huge burden to lay on her. She had no authority over him. He was practically a man, walking around in a man's frame but with the impulse control of a child. She'd need every help possible.

Miranda was gathering vetoes, which eventually got her talking to Parker. Here they encountered their first problem: Parker wanted to veto a song Miranda very much wanted to keep, so she started negotiating. Taken aback, Parker folded his arms and looked irritated. Next Miranda's friends got onboard, and one of them agreed with Parker's veto. Negotiations continued, and finally Parker started to engage.

Mission accomplished. Enrique called, "Time's up! Let's hear the vetoes!"

Eleven songs came off his list. Then Miranda and Parker both voted to add a specific song, so that must have been the outcome of their parlay. Either that or Parker had decided to bail on chorus and pick up trash from the roadside after all.

Enrique recompiled the list. "You guys know some of these, so let's knock out a few standards right now to get a sense of how we sound."

They sang from wherever they were standing or sitting. Enrique walked through the class listening to the first chorus of "Hark the Herald Angels Sing," then began moving the kids around. He made Parker and the other boy stand close enough to hear one another. He separated the two loudest girls with the weakest singer in between them.

Without worrying about harmonizing, the kids belted out the next song just fine. Enrique called out, "Winter Wonderland" and started them off with their third. The kids could do most of these songs without song sheets, but he'd start tracking down music or at least lyrics. He'd work out a couple of showpiece songs, but that would come later. Right now, he wanted them to get a sense of sound and a feeling of community.

When the bell rang for the late bus, Enrique took a quick attendance (with all their real names this time, since they wanted their service hours) and told everyone to come back on Monday.

Parker hung back after everyone had gone. "I sound dumb."

"You don't sound dumb at all. Half of you have no vocal training, but you don't need much. I'll get everyone up to speed in two weeks." Enrique flashed him a smile. "Once everyone starts singing, it's a lot of fun."

"Yeah, I get that." Parker jammed his hands in his

pockets and stared at the smartboard. "Look, I know you're looking out for me because you're dating my sister, but here's the thing. If you hurt her, I don't care that you're my teacher. You don't get to do that to her."

Enrique raised his hands. "I have no intention of hurting Hannah. I've known her for eighteen years, and if I were to act like a jerk to her, you'd only be the first person in line to take a piece out of me."

Startled, Parker glared up.

Enrique folded his arms. "You stood up for her against your stepfather. You're not letting anyone harm her, and that's a good thing because right now, she needs your help."

Parker rolled his eyes. "Like I helped so much."

"You did help because you convinced her how dangerous it was to stay in that house. You did a brave thing, man." Enrique paused. "Dumb, but brave."

Parker laughed despite himself.

Enrique relaxed. "I hope there's not a next time, but if there's another time that brute threatens her, you let me know. It's not just you versus him. It'll be you and me versus him. And you and me and my brother who throws two fifty-pound sacks of flour over his shoulder and wonders if he can grab anything else on the way upstairs. And my brother's firefighter friend who could throw my brother and those two sacks of flour over his shoulder. And, when it comes down to it, the entire police force."

Parker's fists clenched. "Tyler makes me sick. He's worthless and nasty, and I wish he'd go die in a hole."

"People like that don't die in a hole. They keep climbing back out of the hole to torment everyone around them." Enrique folded his arms. "You keep your ears out for anything they might try. If they come, don't let her open the door. If they harass her over text, you tell her to block them. It's the two of you against the two of them, and next they're going to leverage the little kids to rope her back in."

They were already doing it. Enrique had seen the grief in

Hannah's eyes when her mother texted.

Parker shoved his fists in his pockets. "I'm only doing the chorus so I can stay with her. You're telling me you want to protect her, but if you're trying to take advantage of her too, you've got me to deal with."

After all the trouble he was in, was this kid really threatening one of his only allies, just to plant a stake in the ground before his sister's heart? His backbone must be made of stainless steel. Not to mention his ego.

"Duly noted." Enrique opened his hands. "And when you see I'm not a threat to her, I hope you stay in the chorus anyhow, and I hope you keep staying with her. Family is important to Hannah, and right now, you're all the family she's got."

CHAPTER SEVENTEEN

Two guys filled Hannah's mind throughout her days. Parker and Enrique, each with a different schedule, one she needed to look after and one looking after her.

At age fifteen, Parker didn't require feeding or bathing. He barely talked to her. He was out the door for the school bus at 7:15, and she was out fifteen minutes later to drive to work. Hannah did her everyday chores (shopping, cooking, dishwashing) but now she had mental chores. She was always calculating where Parker was and what Parker needed. When she tallied up her list of things to do, she also tallied up his. When she thought about where she should be, she simultaneously knew where he was as well.

This was a lot like playing in a string quartet, come to think of it. Mid-play, she always had to be conscious of what the other three were doing, anticipating any changes, monitoring all the dynamics.

Appointments constantly got added to their schedule.

Parker was required to visit his therapist once a week. There were required calls to Caroline.

Whatever parts of her thoughts Parker didn't fill, Enrique did.

Hannah didn't have to set aside time for Enrique. They texted at random all day long. Well, except for the times he was teaching. Also, not during her busy hours at work. Not during quartet practice (which was now all Christmas music) and never during performances. Come to think of it, Hannah had a whole list of times she couldn't text Enrique, and she kept track of them all. He went between the Hartwell schools, and some afternoons he taught private lessons at the Castleton Music School.

Despite the gaps, it felt like they were talking all day long. It felt good.

Twice a week, the community service chamber group met—and for those two hours, Parker and Enrique were together. Hannah could be conscious of only one location.

Enrique was sweet. She liked thinking about him. It wasn't supposed to happen this way, was it? Or should it have been happening this way all along? It was something she could ask if Caroline ever hooked them up with a family therapist.

Nothing happened quickly. The family therapists, for example, weren't getting back to Caroline in anything like a timely fashion. The hearings for Parker's case were so far in the future that their mother must be losing her mind. The stipend and food assistance were not turning up. Caroline was calm about the molasses-like pace of the process. "If you think this is slow, you should see the criminal justice system." Which, unfortunately, Parker probably would.

On the bright side, Parker liked going to his therapist. "She said I don't have to talk to her, but it'll annoy Mom and Tyler if I spend the whole hour talking about nothing but them. So...I don't know."

"At the very least," Caroline said, "going there makes the case that you're cooperating with the system." To Hannah, she later added, "This therapist is awesome. She uses the first sessions to build rapport. If it helps Parker to think he's rebelling by walking in her door, she'll encourage it."

Caroline, Hannah, and Parker wrote a roommate agreement outlining what Hannah was responsible for, what Parker was responsible for, what she would not do, what he would not do. They set up quiet hours and a chore schedule. "This is stupid," Parker muttered.

"It's stupid until the minute the trash can overflows," said Caroline. "Scheduling chores is boring, but I always advocate for boredom over resentment."

Parker's homework and service hours were part of his agreement. Looking out for him was part of Hannah's.

Hannah told Caroline. "I'd do that anyhow. I've been doing that all my life."

To which Caroline replied, "Now you know you shouldn't have been."

Meanwhile, without a signed agreement, Enrique was looking out for Hannah. He listened to her nerves ahead of the appointments and called afterward to ask how things had gone. She started the calls tentative and ended up laughing. When she felt overwhelmed, he filled her with confidence.

Was this love?

She didn't Google it. Googling what to talk about on a first date hadn't worked, and this question was so much more complicated.

Enrique fascinated her. She'd be grooming a dog and catch herself trying to describe the shade of Enrique's eyes. Driving home, she'd remember his laugh or his touch. She'd repeatedly stop herself from asking if they could meet for five minutes between making dinner for Parker and popping back out the door for quartet practice.

She loved his voice, his touch, his scent. She wanted to cook for him and read to him and play music with him. It didn't matter, though: she'd drive his trash to the dump if it meant they were spending time. Was that love? It was definitely an infatuation. What made love different? Or was growth into love just a matter of time?

What if he didn't love her?

Worse, what if she told him she loved him, only it turned out she didn't? What if her feelings guttered out like a snuffed candle? She wasn't reliable, and she could break his heart. That would be the worst.

They had time. She didn't need to figure it out today or tomorrow. Still, it would have helped to put a name to the feelings. They were dating, but were they a couple? They were getting closer, but was it love?

Enrique invited Hannah to his apartment for dinner on a Saturday night. Parker again bowed out because going there with his sister was gross and creepy. He'd rather eat cereal in his room.

Enrique's apartment was warmer and roomier than Hannah's. Whereas her apartment had been carved from an unused floor of a century-old Victorian, Enrique's building had been designed twenty-five years ago with apartments in mind. The floor plan made actual sense. Everything was convenient and ready to hand.

"It lacks charm," Enrique demurred as he made dinner.

Hannah set the table while he cooked. "Only if you're using an archaic definition of 'charm' that involves cardboard furniture and weird drafts from uninsulated windows."

Enrique checked the oven. "But you have a tin ceiling and designs on the cornices while I've got drywall."

Whereas Hannah had made Enrique mac and cheese, he'd made her French dip sandwiches. Hannah had never seen this before. He cut a loaf of French bread into fist-sized pieces and slathered them with butter, garlic, and salt. Those went under the broiler while he heated up thin slices of roast beef and broth. The whole apartment smelled like garlic and heaven.

"Behold!" Enrique flourished an oval plate. "I own exactly one serving dish!"

She applauded. "Well done!"

"Courtesy of Food Bonanza last summer, if you saved three months of receipts." He plated their meal with style on that one blue dish. He brought out a salad and sparkling lemonade.

Dating Enrique was going to be fun. Hannah hadn't realized you could meet for dinner with no expectations, or text all day to share silly thoughts. Never at any point had she relaxed her guard this much. Always, at every turn, she'd wanted to avoid leading a guy to expect she was more available than she was.

It would be nice to have a metronome for her feelings. Did she love him? Did she not? Did she love him? Did she not?

Enrique had sung that morning for a funeral, but the quartet was in their dry season. Once the tourist influx ended, as the leaves finished falling and the leaf-peepers went home, November went quiet. No one wanted to get married in November. Come December, there would be Christmas parties, but after January first, bookings would dry up again until May. It was the perfect stretch of time to tuck into a cozy apartment, catch up on reading or TV, text a cute guy, and watch the snowfall.

Or maybe not text a cute guy. Maybe hang out at a handsome guy's apartment and snuggle up on the same couch under the same fleece blanket. Maybe listen to music. Maybe more.

When all the plates were empty, Enrique sat back, pleased. "Do you want dessert right away? Or are you stuffed?"

Hannah said, "It's unladylike to admit to that, right?"

"Oh. In that case," and Enrique leaned forward, eyes mischievous, "would my lady care to delay dessert until I am no longer stuffed?"

She tilted her head. "Dear sir, you are too kind. Let's clean up first."

Then it was even fun to wash dishes with Enrique. Was anything not going to be good with him?

Hannah hunted through his cabinets for correct places to set things (his lone serving dish likely ending up on the wrong shelf) and all the time, they were talking. Talking about music, about school, about their schedules. About Bob Castleton. About how Lindsey was struggling to keep the quartet functional under far too much pressure. About the impact on the Castleton family now that Michael had reappeared.

"It's a shame Bob won't get to know Michael." Hannah was drying silverware. "Michael won't meet Bob the way he was, either."

Enrique sighed. "They're getting time together now. That's important."

Hannah said, "Ashlyn says he doesn't recognize Michael. When Susan told him, Bob didn't get it. Last week, he didn't even recognize Ashlyn."

Enrique stared into the sink. "That's got to hurt. Family was everything to Bob. He'd do anything for them."

Hannah said, "Agreed. Which makes it surprising that he and Susan gave up Michael in the first place."

Hands in the soapy water, Enrique didn't move. "Maybe that's because of Michael. Maybe they regretted going through with the adoption plan, and Susan's grief rearranged everything they thought was important."

Hannah wrapped her arms around herself. "Yeah."

"I'm sorry." Enrique dried his hands and stepped toward her. "I didn't mean your family wasn't important."

"Apparently it's not. Parker still doesn't want to see Mom. Mom asked Caroline about a supervised visit, but then Mom didn't follow through. She's texting me guilt trips, but there's no apology."

Enrique wrapped her in his arms, and Hannah rested her temple against his shoulder.

"Mom told me I needed to be there for the family. I

didn't realize it went one way."

Enrique's voice sharpened. "I don't understand her at all."

"She lost my dad, and she lost Parker's dad. To her that meant you could only count on blood, but Tyler isn't blood. At least, not to me or Parker. Not to her."

This was dangerous territory because Enrique had made his opinions clear. Best to pivot. "Susan said when you have kids, you do it with the idea that they'll move away. You're right that it must have crushed Susan to give away Michael."

Enrique squeezed her closer. "A baby makes a relationship permanent. Even if the couple splits, the new person keeps existing."

"Can you imagine that, though? Making a person?" Hannah looked up at him. "That's huge."

He fingered her hair, leaving her tingly all over. "Do you want to have kids?"

"I never thought it possible." She took his hands. "Don't hate my mother. I never expected to get married while she's still alive, and if she thinks a guy would take me away from her, then having kids would have done it even more."

Enrique lowered his voice. "I've heard a baby takes everything you've got."

"You understand." She hugged him. "I hear about one-night stands, and I don't get how anyone can risk that with a stranger. Anyone can want to have sex with you, but making a baby with you? That's a top-grade commitment."

Enrique let go of her hands. "Even so, I'd like to have kids."

Hannah shuddered. "As messed up as I am, I'd be afraid of what I'd do to them."

"You don't have to decide anything. Certainly not now." He kissed her forehead. "Come with me."

In the living room they cuddled on the couch, and he showed her a video of the charity chamber group. Barely opening his mouth, Parker was giving the most lackluster performance of anyone in the history of human song.

Hannah flinched. "I'm sorry."

"He's five times more engaged than the first week." Enrique chuckled. "I took a few videos because I wanted them to see themselves singing so they knew what to correct, but then I decided not to delete them."

Fifteen minutes later, they were still on his couch, Hannah's legs across his lap, his arm wrapped around her back, their heads together. He'd run out of choir clips but was showing her other performances. "Here are the fourth graders, heaven help me." Hannah laughed because they were cute and she only had to watch sixty seconds of video. Enrique kept swiping backward through time. Someone had captured a long video of him performing with Declan Hatcher at a summer festival.

"I want to hear that." Hannah stopped him before he could keep going. "You're so talented, and I love this song."

She snuggled him while they let the video play. If she closed her eyes then the sound would flow through her, but then she wouldn't see Enrique in his tuxedo. He had a few performance quirks he might not realize but which stood out to her as distinctively his. His facial expressions tightened up as he concentrated, not always in sync with the emotions of the song. He concentrated hard for the high notes but looked dreamy for the low ones. It took Hannah two minutes to realize he was singing in Italian, and he didn't speak Italian.

She breathed, "Do you have more of you?"

"I have this one." He went to the index and brought up— the Castleton String Quartet.

"No fair!" She reached for the tablet, but he switched hands and held it just out of reach. "I know what we sound like."

"Actually, this isn't you." He played the video of a wedding, and Hannah gasped.

This was the old quartet: Bob Castleton on first violin, Lindsey on second. Ashlyn played the viola, and Bob's friend Ben played the cello.

Hannah's eyes burned. "Ben stepped down when Lindsey took over. Lindsey was so hurt that he didn't trust her, but Susan promised Ben just wanted Lindsey to put her own stamp on the quartet."

Enrique sighed as the song started up. "He and Bob played together for twenty years, so Lindsey would have bent to him. Stepping out left Lindsey free to shape the quartet."

"I wish he'd stayed." Hannah sighed. "He could have forced Jason to back off when he gets too abrupt. It would have taken a huge burden off Lindsey to have that connection with the past."

"At the expense of the future." Enrique hooked a finger through Hannah's belt loop while the quartet continued playing. "Besides, if he'd stayed, you wouldn't be here."

Enrique's vocals began, but Hannah's brain had switched from enjoyment to analysis. Analysis numbed the ache from watching Bob at the top of his game, or from the longing as she listened to Enrique's song to an unknown bride and groom. The other three instruments backed down while Bob wove his melody line around Enrique's lyrics. Bob had the most musical mind she'd ever encountered...and he was fading out of their lives as early as a December sunset.

Her arm tightened around Enrique. Did he hear the same thing she did? The loss. The longing. The future of the getting-married couple and the destruction of the past quartet?

Hannah murmured, "Send that to me. I want to listen over and over."

Enrique tapped the screen a few times, and Hannah shifted to maneuver her phone from her pocket. She ended up pressed against him, and he snuck a kiss.

"No fair! I wasn't ready." She leaned back, but he followed her down to kiss her again. She snaked her free arm around his shoulders.

A good meal. Good music. And a good guy. This could

get tricky in a hurry, but Hannah felt risky. This time his kiss lingered.

The phone buzzed in her hand. That would be his video, but he pulled back.

Even though he'd given her room, she didn't check her phone. This felt amazing. Maybe it was love after all—the security of his arms around her, the simultaneous vulnerability and invulnerability. His presence filled her senses. His scent. His warmth. Even the sound of his breath and his heartbeat.

If this wasn't love, it was still amazing.

He didn't kiss her a third time, but he did remain near. Silence would have prolonged the moment, but she ought to say something. "I want to play like that for you, the way Bob did. The cello can't give the same contrast to your voice because we're in the same register, but Bob was enhancing your sound."

Enrique sat up, and Hannah fought disappointment as he pulled away. "Bob was incredible, how he could read my mind. Lindsey hasn't quite picked it up yet, and I doubt Jason would even think to do it."

Hannah shifted upright and leaned against him again. "But you and me and the cello—I want to try it. Do you have any instruments here?"

"You can look under the bed, but I'm pretty sure I'd remember having a cello."

Hannah giggled. "Maybe not a cello, but perhaps you've got a grand piano in the medicine cabinet, or a pedal harp in the pantry?"

"Move the big winter coat in the closet and wow, you find an old pair of snow pants and a sousaphone." Enrique paused. "Or, not."

Hannah snickered. "How do you not have an instrument?"

"I have a keyboard in the bedroom, but it's for picking out a melody when I can't figure out on my own what it's supposed to sound like." Enrique sounded uncomfortable. "Next time, bring the cello. Or if you want to try tonight, we could bring dessert back to your apartment and play. I bought cheesecake, so it's portable."

"Parker would love that." Moving, though... She was so comfortable with the blanket and the couch and Enrique close. She could turn just a little toward him and encourage him to kiss her again. Not that she was exactly discouraging him, considering they were wrapped around each other. One song claimed you could tell if a guy loved you with his kiss, but there weren't songs about figuring out whether you loved the guy. Shouldn't you know?

Love shouldn't be confusing. It was innate to human nature. So was music, though, and that could be confusing.

She should tell him. She should tell him she loved him, and then he'd kiss her. He'd know it was love when they kissed, and then he could tell her if he felt the same.

Do it.

Go ahead. Do it. *I love you.* Say it.

Except...not yet. Love needed to be certain, and with the whole world an earthquake beneath her, certain was the last thing she felt.

Hannah's phone buzzed again, three pulses rather than the regular buzz.

Her kid brother's special tone? She struggled to get the phone out and the message onscreen.

"Hannah it's Bentley I need some help please"

She showed Enrique the screen, then pivoted it back to reply.

Enrique put his hand over hers. "Don't answer."

Hannah tugged away. "Bentley needs help."

"That's your mother trying to provoke a response."

"What if Bentley's in trouble?" Bentley wouldn't be alone, so maybe it was really bad. "What if my mother's hurt? What if Tyler went off the rails like he threatened, and Bentley's hiding and scared?"

A second text interrupted her. "Carter is sick and I don't know what to do and he's crying a lot"

Why would Bentley be scared about that? Were there ambulances in the driveway or Mom racing to the hospital with Carter unconscious in the back seat?

Enrique sighed. "Think for a minute. Whoever texted you wrote 'a lot' as two words and correctly used an apostrophe in 'it's'. That's not a kid."

Hannah fought panic and anger. "Bentley dictates into the tablet, and he knows how to make it read messages back to him. We used to play with it all the time, and I set him up a messenger account. That's why there's no punctuation and everything's spelled correctly."

Enrique snorted. "Right. And if he's home with the tablet, why wouldn't he ask your mother or stepfather to help Carter?"

"That's a good question." Hannah dictated her own text into the phone: "Ask Mom for help."

Three dots appeared, followed by the reply. "Mom isn't home"

Enrique said, "And Tyler?"

Hannah sent, "Then ask Dad."

"Dad isn't home I'm scared because he's crying and I can't make him stop"

Enrique huffed. "Tell Bentley to call 9-1-1. That'll end the charade."

Shivering, Hannah sat away from him. "If Carter is really sick but no one's helping him, Mom could be sick too and can't help them."

"Then your kid brother really needs to 9-1-1 so the cops can come and save your sick mother." Enrique's voice had gone flat. "No one's leaving a five-year-old and a three-year-old home alone. If your mother were sick, Bentley would have said Mom was sick, not just Carter. This is a trick to make you break the no-contact order."

It was too late to call Caroline. She wouldn't get the message until tomorrow. Hannah wrung her hands. "I can't take that chance."

"Fine. Whatever. I'll go." Enrique got up from the couch, and Hannah shivered at the loss of his warmth. "You drive back to your apartment with the cheesecake. I'll swing by their house and ring the bell. When your mom opens up, it'll be obvious they were trying to trick you."

Hannah glowered. "How about I save you a trip?" She texted Bentley, "I can't come, but my friend is on his way. He'll make Carter feel better."

Bentley replied, "I'm not allowed to open the door for anyone I don't know"

Enrique snorted. "Oh, that's brilliant."

Hannah took a picture of Enrique. "He looks like this, so now you know him. He will be there in ten minutes."

Bentley replied, "Okay"

"This is manipulation, classic and undiluted." Enrique grabbed his keys, and Hannah got her bag. Two minutes later, they were at Enrique's car. With narrow eyes, he got behind the wheel. "Don't look so upset. I'm going over there because I care about you—and they've got something up their collective sleeves because they *don't*. In twenty minutes, I'll see you for cheesecake." He forced a smile as if he weren't furious. "Cheesecake with a side of annoying Parker."

Hannah wrapped her arms around her waist, more from nerves than the cold. "If Tyler is actually home and you messed up his plans, he's not going to take it well. Be careful. Please."

CHAPTER EIGHTEEN

Enrique glowered as he drove across town. It would help if once, just once, Hannah weren't so fully manipulated by her completely-transparent toxic family members. She'd grown up surrounded by the emotional bludgeoning, so getting yanked around by obligation and guilt felt perfectly normal. She responded with much more suspicion when Enrique treated her with kindness, and that was starting to irritate him.

At 29 Oakview Drive, lights were on all over the bottom floor, and the busted car still sat on blocks. Phone in hand, Enrique rang the bell waiting for the inevitable text from Hannah: *Oh, Bentley has just this very moment messaged that Carter is doing better after all!* Then the kid wouldn't need to open the door. Or maybe the message would say their mother was home, only Bentley hadn't realized she was in the shower. One cross-town drive, wasted.

Ready to leave, Enrique rang again, and the door

opened, exactly one eyeball width. From within came wailing. A little kid peeped up.

Off-balance, Enrique softened his voice. "Are you Bentley? I'm Hannah's friend, Enrique."

The door opened all the way, and the crying grew louder.

Okay, this was odd. Enrique scanned the corners for anyone ready to jump him.

Carter led him into the living room, which stank of vomit. It was all over the carpet. On the couch huddled a smaller version of Bentley, his cheeks pink as if they'd been slapped, his eyes red, and more vomit on his shirt. He was gasping hard and sobbing.

Enrique's mouth went hot. "Where's your mom and dad?"

"They're not coming home for a while. But Carter's sick, and I don't know what to do."

They're not coming home for a while?

Bentley didn't know what to do?

Well, then. Enrique knew what to do. He knew it was time to nail these parents to the wall, and nail them hard. This was beyond manipulative. This was negligent and dangerous.

Enrique knelt alongside the couch to feel Carter's forehead with the thin skin of his wrist, then the back of the kid's neck. He was burning up.

Well, this would look great as Exhibit A in Parker's proceedings, as well as in the Department of Children's Services folders. This would finally convince Hannah her mother didn't have even a hint of the best interests of her children at heart.

"You're all alone?" Enrique needed to be sure before he did this. "For a long time?"

Bentley nodded.

Awesome. No ambiguity here.

"Carter is definitely too sick for you to take care of. I'm going to call some other people to help." Enrique woke his phone with a hard jab from his forefinger. "Where are your mom and dad? Do you know where they went?"

Bentley shrugged. "Out?"

Three button pushes. Nine. One. One.

"What's your emergency?" said a prim voice.

Walking away from the boys, Enrique kept it to just the facts. Two unattended children, one vomiting and with a fever. No, he didn't know if the kid was poisoned or just sick. He didn't know where the parents were. The older boy had called for help. Yes, five years old. Oakview Drive. He stepped outside to double-check the house number, momentarily worried that Hannah's mother's car would pull into the driveway before the cops did.

Enrique poured concern into his voice. "This seems like child neglect." *And the award for Understatement of the Year goes to Enrique Almendarez!* "I need you to send an officer."

The dispatcher assured him someone was on the way.

In the middle of this, Enrique's phone chimed with an incoming text. It would be Hannah. She'd want to know if everything was all right.

Everything was not all right, but once those flashing lights and badges arrived...? Once the cops took the kids and arrested their parents? Then he'd tell her. He'd tell her, finally, everything was all right.

The boys were nervous, but the cops were awesome. "Buddy!" exclaimed the younger officer, kneeling alongside the three-year-old on the couch. "You look like someone who's having a bad day."

Bentley talked to an older officer in the kitchen, and shortly a third officer interviewed Enrique on the porch. He was unamused in a way that lit up Enrique's brain. Yes, these parents would get nailed to the wall. Not even with a nail gun. With spikes. Spikes through the heart. Since they said they weren't upset about losing Hannah and Parker, now they could go right ahead and lose the final two. Served them right.

"Do you know the officer assigned to the previous case?" the cop asked, as though the Hartwell department had more than fifteen officers. A post-it in the locker room should turn up the appropriate person. "I'm thinking we need the sergeant out here."

Enrique thought of Hannah pacing in her apartment, desperate for information. He'd have to tell her soon. Also, now it would be better if he made himself scarce because the cops had the machinery in motion. "You probably don't want me here. In case the parents return."

The officer shared no such urgency. "I need all your information, and you're going to have to talk to child protective services when they arrive."

Fifteen minutes into the process, Enrique got a text from Hannah. "You didn't answer me, and I'm worried. Are they okay?"

About to text a reply, Enrique stopped.

The house was crawling with cops. The cops were trying (and failing) to raise either parent on their cell phones. Carter wasn't seriously sick, probably nothing more than a stomach bug that would resolve with a day in front of the television. Bentley was unhurt, only a little upset— although the longer he talked with the cops, the happier he appeared. He'd be fine too.

Texting Hannah with, "The cops are obtaining a preliminary protection order to remove your brothers from the home" was not going to go over well. By contrast, "Oh, everything's fine" would be...well, true. It would simultaneously be the lie of the century. "You see, the boys were fine once the police arrived and brought them to a place where they wouldn't be left unsupervised."

Everything would be fine. Now the boys would get looked-after. Hannah would get her priorities straightened out. Parker would get his case reviewed in light of the overall neglect. With any luck, Tyler would get pilloried in the court of public opinion. Maybe the mother would get pilloried in the court of Hannah's opinion. Finally. *Finally.*

Hannah needed a response, though. She mustn't come here to answer her own questions. It would be a horror show if the parents returned and found Enrique, but if the parents returned and found Hannah, it was all over. She'd need to make a case to reinstate the no-contact order, and her mother would mount an emotional battle convincing her not to.

Of course, the parents would put it together who called the cops as soon as they looked at the tablet. They might be monsters, but they could read.

Enrique went back into the house. "Ask the boys for their tablet computer. They were messaging their sister Hannah to come help. The whole record should be on there."

Bentley was at the table with an officer, each of them drinking a juice box. He was pleased to unlock the tablet and show the officer how he used dictation software to send texts and read the responses back.

The officer marveled at him. "That's a great tablet, little man! Would you mind if I borrowed it for a bit?"

That would delay the inevitable. Enrique still might want to move in with his brother for a few months. Maybe invest in tactical armor.

Hannah texted again. "Should I come?"

Enrique went to sit on the porch railing, eyes on the street. Neighbors were watching unashamedly from their windows, but it was chilly enough that they weren't gathering on the sidewalk. People had to be taking video. A town this small—a town this boring—and you were guaranteed to draw attention with police cars in the driveway and a sergeant on the way.

With this many neighbors around, why hadn't Hannah's mother left the kids with one of them? Shouldn't people this nosy have volunteered babysitting services just to pump the boys for information about the blow-up with

Parker? Or were they aware of the parents' natures, merely waiting for someone to have the backbone make that call?

Enrique texted Hannah. "The boys are fine. I may be a little while. Carter was vomiting."

Her response: "So they were alone? Bring them here."

He replied, "No, I don't think so. I'll see what happens."

She texted, "They shouldn't be alone."

Wow, would you look at that? Even though she wasn't a mother, Hannah knew little boys shouldn't be left unsupervised.

She texted, "Make Carter toast and weak tea with lots of sugar. That usually makes the boys feel better."

He texted, "Duly noted."

"There should be cans of chicken broth in the pantry. You really should bring them here."

He replied, "I'm not bringing them. It's under control. And you stay there."

Especially now, when her stepfather was most likely to go unhinged.

Her next text appeared. "I don't like this. They must have been so scared."

Enrique sent, "Yeah."

"Tell Bentley and Carter I love them and would be there if I could."

"Will do."

He found Carter on the couch with a blanket and a police officer. "Carter, I was talking to Hannah. She says to tell you she loves you."

Carter got wistful. "I miss Hannah."

"She misses you too." Maybe Caroline could arrange visits with the kids now. "I'll tell her you want to see her."

The front door opened, and he steeled himself in case it was the parents, but it was just a weary social worker. She took note of the smell, the vomit on the carpet, the vomit on the child, and then went into the kitchen to see Bentley. Enrique got paper towels and started cleaning the floor.

Carter said, "I'm sorry."

"You don't need to be sorry. You're sick." What had

Hannah said? "Do you want toast and tea?"

Carter shook his head. The officer looked up from whatever he'd just written. "Let's get you into some fresh clothes, sport."

Carter got off the couch, which was similarly filthy. Enrique didn't bother cleaning that.

The social worker approached with her own list of questions. After he got through the first few, Enrique interrupted with, "Their sister is already acting as guardian for the fifteen-year-old brother. She's asked if she can take these boys too."

The exhausted social worker shook her head. "We're tracking down emergency foster care. Tomorrow we'll get this in front of a judge and get a PPO, but we'll find a place overnight."

Good. A freezing bucket of water in the faces of those two monstrous parents.

Emergency foster care used to be the Castletons' gig. With that rambling house and a regular platoon of kids marching through every day, they'd been naturals at it. Susan was still the kind of person you went to in a crisis. She walked into a room and all at once you felt as if everything were under control. She'd triage what needed to happen and when, and you found the strength to do it.

Still, Hannah would be upset that she or Susan weren't getting the kids. Maybe later. "Do you need me here any longer?"

The social worker got Enrique's contact information, which the police already had anyhow, and Enrique stopped one last time in the kitchen.

"Bentley, my dude, are you going to be okay?"

Bentley nodded. "Officer Joe said Hannah texted me just now. She said she wants to be here, but she's glad you're taking care of me."

Enrique gave him a thumbs-up. "You've got it. Calling was the right thing."

Despite how well this would work out in the end, there would be no celebrating tonight, no cheesecake. Hannah would be worried and sad, but she didn't eat away her emotions. If anything, over the last two weeks she looked even more gaunt than before.

This would finally break Hannah of needing to defend her mother. Her mother had used her. Now that Hannah was gone, and without Parker as the backstop, she'd used no one. In one hard blow Hannah would lose all respect for her mother, but at least Enrique would be there for her to cry on.

CHAPTER NINETEEN

Hannah rushed to the door to find Enrique with his face hard and his eyes dark.

The last she'd heard from him was a vague, "I'm coming back." Had her mother come home? Were the boys with him? She could only assume he was trying to figure out what to do about driving them without their car seats.

Meanwhile, Hannah had done her best to contrive where to put two more boys. Was it kidnapping if she kept them overnight? Maybe Enrique was right and all this was a setup. Hannah had the right to turn away her mother if her mother came for Parker, but not for the little ones.

She pulled him inside. "What happened? Are you alone? Are they okay?"

Enrique had his hands deep in his pockets and his eyes boring through her in a way that left her hair standing on end. "They're okay now."

Parker showed up out of his bedroom. "Did you bring

the bratlings?"

Hannah's pulse went through the roof. "Parker!"

"No? Fine." Parker slammed the door.

Enrique snickered. "I think that's a normal reaction to having siblings ten years younger."

"I didn't treat Parker that way." Hannah hugged Enrique. "Thank you for going over there. They really needed you. You stayed until my mother and Tyler got back?"

His voice went flat. "They weren't back when I left."

Hannah's eyes widened. "You left them alone?"

He recoiled. "Of course not! This whole thing started because it was dangerous if they were alone!"

Reeling, she said, "So who's with them? Did my stepfather threaten you?"

"No, Hannah, wait. Stop." Enrique looked around, and Hannah realized he wanted to sit and talk, but the kitchen was still unfurnished. She brought him to the futon, but as he sat ramrod straight, his tension left her wanting to crawl the walls.

He took a deep breath, and he disengaged. He became a teacher, and his delivery changed to something more calculated. "When Bentley let me in, Carter was on the couch. He'd been vomiting, and it was all over the carpet and all over his clothes. Bentley didn't know what to do."

Hannah wrapped her hands around each other. "Had Mom run to the store to get meds?"

"Your mom and Tyler were out for the night. Bentley had been calling them for a while, which is why he messaged you. He didn't know when they'd be back, but he guessed they'd been gone at least an hour."

Hannah bit her lip. "Bentley's not good with time. He'll say something's been hours when it's been five minutes. If he's been having fun, it's only minutes."

"It wasn't five minutes. Carter had vomited in at least two places on the carpet and again on the couch." Enrique was beyond tense. "Your mother abandoned them. I called the police."

Hannah jolted back. "But they're already in trouble with

the cops!"

Enrique folded his arms. "Not my problem. My job was looking out for the kids, so I had no choice."

"Of course you had a choice! The phone didn't dial itself! Did you tell them you wanted an ambulance because a kid was puking?" Hannah got to her feet. "Do you have any idea how much trouble you just created?"

Enrique looked up, irritated. "I created the trouble?"

"There wouldn't have been trouble if you hadn't called the cops!"

"Do you know how else there wouldn't have been trouble?" He glared at her. "If your mother and stepfather had thought for five seconds before leaving two little boys alone for the night."

She was so angry it was hard to think. "That's not the point!"

"Of course it's the point! It's negligent to leave a kindergartener in charge of a preschooler! That's why I needed the cops."

"You could have stayed with them until someone came home! You could have brought them here. Then it wouldn't be neglect because they'd have been with adults."

Enrique glowered. "And then what?"

"Then we'd have called Caroline tomorrow or Monday and asked her get my mother's side of the story."

Enrique's eyebrows contracted. "Don't worry. Based on what the cops said, lots of people will ask for her side of the story."

"But cops! Where are the boys now? When my mother came home, didn't she—"

"She didn't!" Enrique stood. "Can't you hear what I'm saying? I was there almost an hour, and they never came home. Neither of them answered their phones. There wasn't a neighbor checking on the boys. Your brothers were entirely alone! One of them sick, one of them terrified."

Parker came out of his room, breathing hard. Hannah's cheeks burned.

"You should have brought them here." Her voice broke. "It's not like they were dying. I could have sat up with Carter."

Enrique stared, his expression a swirl of anger and defeat.

"I could have helped them." She wrapped her hands around each other. "Where are they now? The police station?"

Parker huffed. "Overnight in the lockup! Awesome place for little kids."

Enrique glared from Parker to her. "A social worker came. She's sending them to emergency foster care overnight so they can get in front of a judge in the morning. I did ask for the boys to come here, but she didn't want to send the kids to you overnight."

Rage boiled inside Hannah. For the first time in her life, she wanted to hit someone.

Parker huffed. "I hope both of them get arrested. It's about freaking time."

Enrique's eyes sparked. Was he enjoying this? Didn't he realize he was relishing her family's detonation?

Hannah looked at him again. No, he did realize. He realized, and he didn't care.

She understood Parker's anger, but Enrique had nothing to be angry about. "If you hadn't called the cops, you wouldn't have had to ask anyone for permission."

Enrique's voice was flat. "I saw neglect. I'm a teacher. That makes me a mandatory reporter."

She threw out her hands. "And that means?"

"The state requires me to report any suspected child abuse or neglect. I'd lose my job if I didn't call when I saw two endangered children. That's what it means."

He was so cold. So calculated. So— So not the Enrique she'd begun to love.

Hannah's eyes narrowed. "And your job is more important than my family? After all the stuff you were just telling me about how important family is? You wouldn't even drive my brothers a mile and a half?"

The anger on Enrique's face grew more pronounced, but he lowered his voice to nearly a breath. He had great tonal control. Of course he did. He was using it like a surgeon's scalpel. "Hannah. The kids. I was acting to save the kids."

Parker was dead silent. Hannah's hands clenched. "Saving them by destroying their home?"

Enrique squared his shoulders. "Yes, it was me. I destroyed everything. I'm the one who convinced your stepfather to stalk you, and I made your stepfather threaten you in front of Parker. I convinced your mother against her better judgment to see a movie while her toddler vomited on the couch. It was all me." Enrique's hands clenched. "The social worker had nothing to do with it. The cops? All my playthings. For that matter, I wrote the state statutes."

He stalked to the door.

Hannah shouted, "You don't get to drop a bomb in my family's lap and walk away!"

Enrique yanked open the door. "Then call the cops on me for neglecting my bomb," and he slammed it behind him.

Enrique's footsteps descended the wooden staircase, and Hannah ran to go after him.

Parker jumped in front of the door. "Seriously, don't. You're going to scream in the street like a banshee. It won't change a thing, and you'll look like a crazy lady."

She tried to get around him. "Let me go!"

Parker jammed his back against the doorknob. "Don't! He's leaving, and if you yell at him, he's going to tell you again he had no choice, and you'll get madder and keep shrieking at him, and then someone gets to call the cops on us too."

Hannah backed off. "He did have a choice!"

Parker glowered. "He already blew it up, and you howling like a coyote isn't going to undo it."

Everything was destroyed. Mom would have no kids. Tyler would go berserk. The little ones would be terrified in some stranger's house. They probably wouldn't even get to keep the tablet computer so they could contact her. Mom would have no one at all.

Hannah was supposed to be the one who never caused any trouble, and she'd been stupid enough to fall in love with a guy who'd caused a mountain of trouble on her behalf. She never should have gone on a date with Enrique, never should have let him kiss her, never should have started texting him and calling him. Shouldn't have fallen in love. Shouldn't have, shouldn't have, shouldn't have.

Parker said screaming wouldn't undo it, but Hannah wanted so badly to scream, scream, scream until her throat bled and her eyes stung, and finally the world would give up in the face of her tantrum, reversing course so none of this would have happened. Skip backward a few weeks so she could pluck the errant phone from Cashman's hands. Deliver a prim, "Thank you, but I'll handle this," and walk out the door. Let Tyler invade her privacy forever and ever, and then her mother wouldn't lose all four of her children.

Parker didn't unguard the door. Enrique would have driven off by now. Hannah couldn't see the street to be sure.

Parker kept his arms folded. "Stop and think. When Mom and Tyler get home, the cops will be there. What will they do?"

Hannah's breathing shuddered in her throat. "Get arrested?"

Parker shook his head. "The cops said they don't like people in the lockup overnight. It's just more work for them. I'm betting the cops sit them down and have the social worker explain the laws and then try scaring them."

They'd scared Hannah, and she wasn't even there.

Parker frowned. "I hope the cops know manipulation when they see it. Mom's going to cry."

Hannah breathed, "Tyler's going to come here."

Of course he'd come to her. She'd bet the house (well, the house she didn't have) that by now Tyler had figured out where she and Parker lived. He'd have had a friend follow her home from work or tail Parker home from school.

Tyler would bang on the door and threaten them. He'd believe the little ones were inside, and while he didn't care what happened to Parker, he wouldn't let Hannah steal his own blood.

Hannah murmured, "If they come here, I'm calling the cops. That's what Susan said—since the law's on our side, use it like a club."

The cops wouldn't mess around, but what if they took a while to get here? What if Tyler tried to hit Parker or broke her cello or...?

Parker looked around the kitchen. "What do we have for weapons?"

If they were improvising weapons, they had to get away. Hannah pulled out her phone. "That's a bad plan. We need better advice."

Thirty seconds later, she had Susan Castleton on the phone, and Susan's voice brought immediate light into Hannah's head. "Deep breath. First of all, you're not responsible for this."

Susan was on speakerphone, propped on the futon, while Hannah knelt on the floor and Parker stood in the hallway with his baseball bat.

"You're not at fault for sending Enrique to the house, and you're not at fault for your mother and stepfather abandoning the little ones. You were concerned about them, and that was the right thing."

Hannah said, "Even if I was right, Tyler is going to blame us."

Parker said, "If he comes here, I'm going to kill him."

"Parker, if he goes to your apartment, call the cops and

let the cops gun him down. Keep your hands clean." Susan was so...factual. Hannah kept leaning on that because her own compass was spinning like an oscillating fan. "I'm not sure Tyler knows where you live. Unless there's an immediate threat, the social workers usually disclose the kids' locations, so he'll know they aren't with you."

Parker snorted. "It's not about getting the kids. It's about getting revenge. He's jealous of anyone and everything. If you so much as think about criticizing him, or if you even do something different from him, it's an insult that he needs to get back at you for. He'll be embarrassed and angry, so he'll blame Hannah and come looking for her."

Susan said, "Do you want to stay here?"

Hannah fought vertigo. "That endangers you, and you have more to lose."

Susan said, "He won't threaten me because he'll know he can't pull the obligation card. If you want to stay here, stay here."

Hannah said, "But what about my mother?"

Parker exclaimed, "For crying out loud, who cares about Mom?"

Hannah blinked hard. "I care about Mom!"

Susan sighed. "Your mother needs to deal with this on her own. She made the decision. She lives with the consequences."

Hannah shook her head. "I should have been watching the kids."

"Your mother was not unaware that you moved out. Her decisions are on her."

Hannah lowered her face onto her crossed arms. "You know the laws are crazy. Moms lose their kids for leaving them in a parked car for two minutes to buy milk at the convenience store."

Susan's voice picked up an edge. "This is not the same, and you know it. Your only concern right now is keeping Parker safe."

Parker said, "And if he comes in here, I'm killing him."

"If he comes there, you keep the door locked. You report a home invasion in progress and tell 9-1-1 he's going to kill you."

Parker said, "I'll lock Hannah in her bedroom, and I'll take him down in the kitchen."

"In the meantime," Susan said, overriding Parker's dreams of glory, "one of you could phone the police to remind them there's a restraining order in place, and add that the man may go unglued. Tell them you want extra patrols on your street."

Parker said, "Because Tyler is totally stupid and would park Mom's car right in front of this house, then stand outside until the hourly police drive-by?"

Susan sighed. "What do you want to do?"

Hannah lifted her head. "Parker, do your friends know where we live? Your friends' parents? If he or Mom calls any of them, would they tell them where we live?"

Parker pulled out his phone. "I'll tell them to keep it a secret. Actually, I'll tell them to pretend I took a bus to Lewiston for the weekend."

"Have them notify you if they get that call," Susan said.

Parker added, "Tyler doesn't even know who my friends are."

Hannah said, "Mom knows."

Parker looked up from his phone long enough to side-eye her. "If Mom helps Tyler get our address so he can beat us up, then I hope they both get the death penalty."

Hannah fought nausea. This wasn't fair. Everyone was so angry, and no one was thinking clearly.

Susan said, "Executive decision time. I'm going to drive over there, and you two get in my car. Hannah, keep a light on in your apartment, and leave your car where it's nice and visible. If he comes, he'll think you're home. He'll break in and maybe trash the place, or maybe trash your car, but he won't harm you."

Hannah shuddered.

"Let your landlady know anything she hears is not you, so call the police." Background sounds came through the phone. "I'll be there in five minutes. Be ready to get in my car."

Hannah said, "Can I bring my cello?" to which Parker rolled his eyes so hard. But her cello was the most valuable possession she had.

Susan said, "The cello and all your electronics. In the morning we'll devise a better plan."

Parker said, "And then on Monday, I take care of Enrique?"

Susan said, "On Monday, you leave Enrique alone because he did exactly what he was supposed to do."

Hannah said, "Enrique's the cause of all this trouble!"

Susan fell totally silent.

Hannah said, "I trusted him, and he called the cops."

The speakerphone thunked with the sound of a car door shutting. "Make it through the rest of the weekend, and next week, when everyone's calmer, then we can discuss Enrique."

CHAPTER TWENTY

Enrique never should have gotten involved.

He compulsively glanced in the rear-view mirror every twenty seconds, but this was Hartwell. Anyone tailing him home would have been visible. Also, why tail him? Anyone who could install spyware could also type "Enrique Almendarez" into a search engine and come up with his address.

He was an idiot. When he saw the train wreck that was Hannah's life, instead of feeling warm and protective, he should have backed away with wide eyes and a nervous smile. He shouldn't have noticed how beautiful she was and should instead have noticed how she'd been gaslit into believing these people were normal. Believing they loved her.

She had no idea what love was. If she ever felt the real thing, she'd wonder what it was and then decide it was fantasy. If someone gave her unconditional love, she'd believe it was dangerous.

At his apartment, he made sure the door locked behind him. He texted Daniel. "I'm coming to your house."

His brother replied, "This sounds fun. Are we going back out again? Because I've got to be up for church at nine."

Enrique texted back, "This is no fun at all, and at this point, I may go to church with you."

He stuffed things in an overnight bag and scanned the halls and the stairs and the parking lot like a Mafia defector—even checked beneath his car. This was crazy.

His sister-in-law led Enrique straight into the kitchen where she had a kettle boiling on the stove. "Tea? I have no idea what's going on, but tea or hot chocolate seemed like an idea." She hugged Enrique. "I'll get the spare room set up, but make whatever you want."

Daniel sat at the table. "What happened that's about to lead you back to Jesus?"

Enrique rolled his eyes. "I need someone to talk sanity to me."

Daniel folded his arms. "That sounds like a coffee problem rather than a hot chocolate problem."

Enrique huffed. "Make it super hot so I can throw it at someone."

By the time Enrique was done with the story, Daniel's eyes were narrow and dark. When Sharon returned, he waved her over to sit with them. At the end, with his hands wrapped around the mug of instant coffee, all of it still in the mug and none of it inside him, Enrique said, "Am I losing my mind? Did I do the wrong thing?"

Daniel huffed. "Don't question it for a moment."

Sharon added, "Your girlfriend—Hannah?—she's not thinking clearly because she's distraught. If you'd made a ridiculous call to the police, the police wouldn't have involved a social worker. The dispatcher wouldn't even have sent an officer."

Laughing, Daniel shook his head. "Nothing happens in this town, and all the cops are bored. I'm surprised they didn't send a fire truck too."

"But after the cops had their excitement, they'd have gone away." Sharon bit her lip. "Are you sure the parents didn't get into a car accident? If they weren't answering their phones, maybe they're both dead."

Enrique frowned. "By the time the system chews them up and spits them out, they'll wish they were dead."

Daniel waved a hand. "Not a chance. They'll go in front of a judge and plead stupidity. They'll take a couple of parenting classes where the instructor will say in small words that a five-year-old shouldn't babysit a three-year-old, and they'll nod sagely while thanking the system for this valuable education. With all the boxes checked, they'll get the kids back. That's assuming they don't get them back Monday afternoon without jumping through any hoops at all."

Sharon pursed her lips. "I can't believe that."

Enrique's shoulders slumped. "He may be right. I've heard about students in worse situations who didn't get taken. Parker's only with Hannah because the mother rejected him."

Daniel glowered. "That family is a disaster. Break up with the girl and get out of there."

With a huff, Enrique stared off to the side.

Break up with Hannah. They were barely even going out. It would be easiest now, when neither of them had any real investment. He hadn't even told half his friends. They'd kissed a few times and eaten a few meals together. He'd hauled her boxes. They could be done.

It would be awkward at first, but he'd dated other musicians and still worked with them—including, hilariously, Lindsey Castleton. A few dates followed by an amicable breakup once they agreed the chemistry was basically water and gold: nothing happened. You didn't even get rust.

Hannah, though... They did have chemistry. He could feel his humor mixing with hers, her personality brightening under his influence, his heart lightening with her adoration. She was entranced with him—although maybe not anymore—and the more they talked or texted, the more she kept being entranced. He'd begun looking forward to the times they could meet, daydreaming about past kisses and anticipating future ones. Her presence warmed him. Her touch thrilled him.

Enrique's hands clenched on the mug. "Her family's bonkers, but I don't want to do that yet. I'm here mostly because when her stepfather learns I'm the one who made the call, he may decide I'm fair game."

Daniel's eyes widened. "Dude, if the man's that unstable, why'd you leave Hannah alone?"

Enrique shrugged. "She was going to argue with me for as long as I stuck around. Besides, she has a restraining order."

Daniel snorted. "A restraining order is a piece of paper. If the guy grabs his shotgun to kill her, he's not going to think twice just because it's illegal to be within four hundred feet."

Sharon added, "Ted says the only purpose of a restraining order is to identify the murderer."

Enrique's eyes flared. "You think she's in danger?"

Daniel leaned forward. "Bro, you think you're in danger. How could she not be?"

Blast it. He'd messed this up. He'd walked away without thinking.

Daniel drummed his fingers. "She's got that kid with her, too. Bad move. You needed to let her scream until she wore herself out, then camp in front of her door with a knife under your pillow."

Enrique hunched forward until his shoulder blades met. "The stepfather doesn't know where she lives."

"Yeah, the spymaster general had every device of hers bugged five ways to Sunday, but he doesn't have her address? Get a clue."

Daniel didn't need to be nasty. There wasn't any way to know what Tyler knew or didn't know. Or what the social workers had let slip. Or if it was written in any documentation that he'd read upside-down on their desks.

Sharon reached for her phone. "You want her to come here?"

Enrique shook his head. "You've got your own kid to think about."

Daniel flexed his shoulders. "Frankly, if that slimeball shows up, I wouldn't mind getting a piece of him. My house, my self-defense. He'll spend the next five days with ibuprofen and ice packs wondering why he ever thought it was a good idea."

His brother looked eager. Enrique only wished he felt that confident in a fight. "Fine, I'll text her."

He sent, "I'm not sure you're safe in that apartment. My brother and his wife said you guys can stay with them."

He'd just fail to mention he was staying here too. Or if she freaked out, maybe he wouldn't stay.

Hannah replied, "Not necessary."

Enrique muttered, "'Not necessary.' Yeah, endanger yourself because you're mad at me. That's brilliant."

Sharon frowned. "Why do you think she's still mad at you? She sounds restrained."

"Coming from her, that's blinding fury." Enrique texted, "What's your plan if he comes to the door?"

Hannah replied, "I said we're okay."

With his stomach like a rock, Enrique put down the phone. He shouldn't have left. She was being fatally stubborn.

Unless she'd gone to Susan's. That made sense. Gone to Susan's...and didn't want to say so in case her psycho stepfather still had access.

Enrique wrote back, "I'm leaving my phone on. Call if anything changes."

No response.

No response, and everything inside him went to dust when he realized he didn't expect to get one again.

CHAPTER TWENTY-ONE

On Monday, Hannah trudged to work with a lump in her throat and a dozen messages on her phone, plus calls in to Caroline and to Parker's therapist.

Dr. Griffin got one look at her. "Rough weekend? Did you sleep at all?"

Hannah shook her head. "I'm mainlining coffee to make it through. Maybe it'll be an easy day."

Hah, what a joke. Mondays at the clinic were always rough. With all the Sunday emergencies and half the Saturday emergencies calling in, they were guaranteed a full schedule, plus extra appointments "worked in" wherever they could fit. Kitty burned her paws on the woodstove. Rex cornered a badger and got his nose slashed. Fluffy is listless in her hutch and hasn't eaten for thirty-six hours.

In the middle of all this, Hannah picked up messages. Oh, look, a text from Mom: Mom wanted Hannah to get the littles and swear to Caroline it wasn't her mother's fault, that her mother hadn't abandoned them. Oh, and also the reminders that if Hannah hadn't left home, this wouldn't have happened.

It was true: Hannah should have been there. Usually, she was.

On the other hand, Caroline texted point-blank that Hannah would not be getting the little ones. "Most likely their parents will get them back this afternoon under certain conditions. Regardless, your apartment doesn't have enough bedrooms, and Parker needs your focus."

Hannah replied, "I can make it work."

Caroline said, "Of course you can. Parker has a history of violence, though, even if it's only violence against property. The judge will most likely return the boys to their parents, and in two weeks, they'll have a formal hearing."

Hannah said, "My mother is desperate."

To which Caroline replied, "You should have blocked her. Under no circumstances should you reply to anything."

It was hard, though. Hard not to reply when her mother was by turns despairing, angry, and lost.

Parker's therapist was much more practical. "I've got an opening tonight at five."

Sure, why not bring Parker? It wasn't as if Hannah had anyone else to see.

Thinking of Enrique left Hannah nauseated and unsteady. For what seemed like weeks she'd been thinking of Enrique all the time. Now she'd reflexively think of him and want to retch. She'd think about his betrayal. About the way she'd been so close to telling him she loved him, and then he'd proven he had no love for her. He'd promised to take care of things and then blown those very things to shrapnel. He'd been encouraging her to destroy her family from the moment he heard about the spyware.

Thinking of Enrique hurt too much. Instead Hannah did some phone work, and third on the list was Cashman

Lavera, owner of the creature formerly known as Not Really My Cat.

"Good afternoon," Hannah said with feigned brightness. "This is Hannah Staples from Brighthead Veterinary Hospital, and I was calling about Braddy."

Cashman said, "Do you want me to put him on the phone?" and she laughed. She couldn't remember the last time she'd laughed. "Braddy seems fine. He still loathes me, but he's hardly alone in that."

Hannah's brow furrowed. "Loathes you?"

"He'll sit on the opposite side of the couch and *stare*. It sounds like he's purring, but the whole time he's flexing his claws, nice and threatening-like. Therefore, we have an understanding. I stay over *here*, and he stays over *there*, and under this arrangement the claws and I don't make a brief but regrettable acquaintance. He does understand that talking is verbal contact, though, and he tolerates that."

Hannah bit her lip. "Actually, when they're flexing their claws—"

"Yes, I know, I know. I've discovered that if you have a question about cats, like why your cat is so pleased to threaten you, all you have to do is post a picture of the cat and ask the question. Four million internet users will subsequently volunteer the answer."

He sounded amused. Hannah said, "So you're adjusting okay?"

"Not at all. You in no way warned me how weird it is to walk into your house and find an animal in it." Again, he didn't sound as irritated as his words indicated. He did sound distracted, as if talking while working. "You were right about him deciding this was the better life. Cat lived in a parking lot for four years, and now he has a squishy bed and a bowl that says 'Poor Starving Cat.' He's expressed no interest in finding the door."

She snickered. "Yeah, he didn't seem like a feral to me. Someone probably had him as a kitten and then dumped him."

Cashman huffed. "Humans. Why do they do that?"

Why indeed? Why would someone drive a cat into the middle of the woods and leave it starving and afraid, telling themselves, "Oh, it'll be all right"? Because people were massive jerks who convinced you to love them and then ditched you the moment it convenienced them to do so.

Instead, she said, "Maybe the former owner moved, and Braddy just wasn't cute enough to keep. Maybe he was spraying the corners. Maybe the previous owner got pregnant."

"Pregnancy?" Cashman sounded surprised. "Why would that matter?"

"Toxoplasmosis." Preoccupied, she was running down the record in front of her to make sure to get all the follow-up questions. "There's also a myth that cats 'steal the baby's breath away,' but they don't."

"Good to know. I'll look that up."

Googling myths not to believe: must be a computer tech thing.

Before she could ask about Braddy's recovery, Cashman said, "By the way, I'm having a fantastic time with your former phones. The spy software survived two factory resets, so I gave your phone and your brother's their own private Wi-Fi network to play with. It's a sealed sandbox that doesn't connect to the internet, but both phones think it does. Every so often I'll play music or take a picture just to provoke the software to respond while I record everything the phone tries to upload and where it tries to upload to. They're both reporting to the same account, so it's not random. Whenever you're ready to press charges, I have a mountain of data to amuse the District Attorney's office. I've never been a witness in a court case, but I think that will give me a certain clout around Brighthead. *Cashman Lavera, Expert Witness.*"

Everyone thought of Hannah's family's turmoil as entertainment. Did guys live for that one victorious moment, when they bounded onto the rooftop like a caped superstar but never turned their heads to tally up the collateral damage? Enrique must have had fun being the big hero who saved the two little children.

Hannah sighed. "I don't think I'm going to press charges. They're leaving me alone."

The background noises resumed. "How cruel. First you gave me a cat, and then you deprived me of the chance to testify."

She leaned back in her chair. "I also stole your GPS detector. When I moved, your wand got put somewhere, and I'm not sure where."

"Not a problem. It's not exactly in everyday use."

Hannah said, "It may take a few days."

"Still not a problem. I bought it after you showed up because half of Reddit convinced me it would be cool to sweep for tracking devices everywhere I went. I'd already annoyed everyone in Brighthead, and there isn't exactly a line of customers asking since then."

"Oh." She bit her lip. "I'm causing quite a bit of trouble, aren't I?"

"I'm not sure how you're decoding any of what I said that way." Cashman paused. "Anyhow, Braddy eats the pill treats, although after he ran out of pain meds, he was annoyed to get fewer treats. This morning he managed to eat the treat around the pill so I had to re-wrap the pill in a second treat. This may end badly."

She laughed. "You guys are doing fine. Thank you for looking more into the phone."

Cashman said, "Not a problem. Let me know when you find the detector or if you need the phones and the data log handed over as evidence."

Again, everyone wanted to involve the police in her family. Evidence, charges, testimony, hearings, custody, stalking—why did it have to be so complicated? Everyone's family had problems. The cops didn't have to storm in every time a family got into a tricky situation.

Cashman she could understand. He was a stranger approaching her technical issues from a business perspective. Enrique? He should have known better. As a teacher he'd seen all sorts of family troubles. His own family was important to him. He should have, should have, should have known better.

By the time Hannah got to quartet practice on Tuesday, she wasn't sure she'd be able to play due to exhaustion.

Jason wasn't there yet, but Lindsey and Ashlyn both looked up at her with concern. Lindsey said, "Wow. Are you alive at all?"

Ashlyn said, "What she means is, you look strung out."

Hannah retreated into her heart. "It's been a long day."

Lindsey said, "Has your stepfather left you alone? The situation is so messed up."

Ashlyn shook her head. "Look, parents are people, and people mess things up. If the kids needed to be out of the house, then it's better that everyone gets a wake-up call."

Hannah started unpacking her cello. "The kids are back home."

Ashlyn muttered, "Of course they are."

Hannah looked up at her. "What?"

Ashlyn rolled her eyes. "I got ping-ponged that way too. 'Your mother isn't safe, Ash, so stay here.' 'Wait, the judge said she's safe.' 'Oops, she's not safe after all, so come with us.' 'Hold on, she took a parenting class, so she's safe again.' The boomerang derby didn't end until the Castletons took me."

Hannah paused. "I didn't realize that. I knew you stayed with them, but not everything before."

Ashlyn's eyes narrowed. "Yeah, and it was a long 'before'. The state will tell you until the sun falls out of the sky that their goal is to reunite families, but my mother was unstable. Sometimes it's just not a good idea."

"Well, my mother isn't unstable. My stepfather may have issues, but he didn't go violent on anyone over the weekend. The only thing that happened was we created a ton of paperwork."

Jason walked in just as Lindsey started tuning. She said, "I love creating paperwork."

Jason rested a hand on his heart. "I too love paperwork. Particularly contracts and checks. Have we generated a mountain of those this week?"

Lindsey brightened. "Actually, yes! The Friends of the Library have once again contracted us to play their holiday party. Last year they got to hear my dad's lineup, and this year, they get to compare us to the splendid musicians who've gone before."

Jason stripped off his winter jacket. "Awesome. Now I can afford stamps for my Christmas cards."

Ashlyn said, "Both of them?" and Lindsey spit out a laugh.

Jason side-eyed her. "Well, now you're off the list, so I can save a stamp."

Lindsey pouted. "That's a bummer. I figured you would send everyone a photo of your pretty face as the true meaning of Christmas, and then I could thumbtack it to my wall."

Jason gave her a thumbs-up. "Tape it to the mirror instead so when you're brushing your teeth, you can meditate on the greatness to which you aspire," which left Ashlyn in a fit of giggles.

Lindsey just stared at him. "Thank you for clarifying my aspirations."

Hannah only got to work tuning her cello. This was a waste. She might as well go home.

"A useful service I provide." Jason turned to Hannah. "Oh, and Hannah, can you just *shut up?*"

Hannah's head jerked up.

Ashlyn huffed. "Cut her some slack. She's super stressed, and the mountain of paperwork we were discussing is actually her mountain."

Chagrined, Jason said, "Sorry. You're always so quiet."

Hannah said, "It's okay," even though it wasn't.

Jason said to Lindsey, "Give me whatever tone you're calling an A tonight," and he tuned.

Ashlyn said, "What else do we have on the docket for Christmas?"

Lindsey ran down a list of performances: holiday parties, tree-lightings, and one mid-day school function that would require time off from work.

Jason said, "Three performances the Saturday before Christmas, and two on the Sunday? Well, that craters the whole weekend."

Ashlyn paged through her sheet music. "Hardly. We can fit one more Sunday performance, plus two on Friday night if we break the speed limit in between. Or if you drive like normal."

Jason grimaced. "Have you figured out yet which one is the gas pedal?"

Ashlyn beamed. "Once I do, I'll let you know which one is the brake."

Lindsey said, "Also, one of the churches wants us to perform ahead of their midnight Christmas Eve service, but I haven't agreed yet. It's a great opportunity, but we'd be onboard from eleven to midnight, and I didn't know if you'd all be okay with that. Enrique's already signed on to cantor the service."

Ashlyn shot a smile at Hannah. "With Enrique there, how can we say no?"

Nauseated, Hannah looked away.

They'd have to perform together at some point. The music community was too small for it never to happen. But so soon?

You had to trust your fellow musicians. You needed to know they'd come in on cue, at the right volume, at the right time. You needed to trust they would correct for their mistakes as well as yours. She used to trust Enrique.

Jason sounded cautious. "Playing until midnight is fine, but do we have to stay for the service after?"

Ashlyn put a hand over her mouth. "And skip out on Jesus's birthday party? How rude."

Lindsey shrugged. "You can go home and wait for Santa, you filthy heathen."

"Guys!" Hannah glared up, hands trembling. "Would you quit it with the insults and the fighting? I can't deal with it tonight."

All three others fell silent.

Ashlyn managed, "Sorry," even though she was the least of the problems.

Jason recoiled. "What's actually wrong?"

"Everything is actually wrong!" Hannah stared at him, then at Lindsey. "We're here to practice, and you two turn everything into a war zone. How about we play? Tune up. Rehearse the songs. Get out. How hard is this?"

Jason raised his hand. "Truce."

Lindsey nodded. "Truce."

Ashlyn said, "Truce here too. I didn't mean to get on your nerves. Just because my story worked out one way doesn't mean yours will work out the same."

Hannah straightened her sheet music on the stand. "Can we get started?"

Lindsey gave a quiet, "Sure," and then told them which song to play.

Everything was an irritation, from Ashlyn's slightly-flat C string to Jason's perpetual upstaging of the first violin line. Lindsey's subdued comments after they finished were as obnoxious as her fighting with Jason. It was an act. They were going to pretend at peace as if Hannah were a harpy who'd unleash her claws at the first opportunity. The fighting was still there, just buried.

Lindsey suggested the next song, her voice way too quiet.

Hannah hated all this. Hated being trouble, hated being bowled over by other people causing trouble. Hated being invisible and then hated being seen. Hated how the other three could mess around and make mistakes, but the one time she asked for something, something they should have been doing from the start, everyone acted like it was a major issue.

At the end of the piece, Lindsey said, "We're going to play through that one again. Jason, slightly less volume. Ashlyn, before I lose my mind, please check your tuning."

"The C string won't stay tuned. I thought I could get another few days out of it, but it's going wobbly." She kept the viola tucked under her chin while adjusting the microtuner with her right hand and picking the string with her left.

Jason said, "Should we leave off the Christmas stuff and run through the lineup for the Thanksgiving Day party?"

The plight of the musician: you never got to celebrate any actual holidays because you were helping other people celebrate theirs. Hannah was used to it, but this Thanksgiving and Christmas, Parker would have nowhere to go.

Lindsey said, "Sure, but I wanted a quick review of the Christmas pieces so I could decide which ones needed work. Speaking of Thanksgiving, though, I've got an invitation for everyone. Since my family's Thanksgiving is in ruins, my mother's hosting an open house with heavy appetizers on Thursday evening, and we'll do the big meal on Sunday instead. Turkey, stuffing, the works."

Ashlyn smirked. "This sleight-of-hand also enables Mom to have Michael at her Thanksgiving dinner without creating even a hint of a schedule conflict with his parents."

Lindsey raised her eyebrows. "My mother is naturally diplomatic in a way most lifelong ambassadors would sell their souls to achieve. Regardless, that's our schedule, and she told me to invite all of you to both."

Lindsey was pointedly not looking at Jason. Jason only said, "I've got plans, but thank her for the invitation."

Relieved, Lindsey turned to Hannah.

Hannah said, "I'll talk to Parker. The community choir may be singing that weekend."

Assuming Parker still wanted to sing. But he had to. He

needed the service hours.

Just...how do you trust your choir director about timing and volume and emphasis when he's proven he'll undermine your work?

Trust was a big deal with multiple voices, in choruses as well as quartets. Sometimes your part alone sounded terrible, but blended in with the others it was amazing. Not "fixing" or adjusting your part meant you trusted the director to have the overall good of the piece in mind, even if it meant you were playing low or dissonant or not at all. Lack of trust harmed the music. It harmed everything.

Given what Enrique said about the chorus, maybe he wasn't looking for great dynamics. Maybe he just wanted them all to sing the same song in the same key. At the same time, even.

"Well, Enrique's invited too, so let him know." Lindsey pulled a notebook from her bag. "The Thanksgiving playlist isn't that different from our wedding reception playlists, and we're performance-ready on every one of those."

Jason smirked. "'Here Comes the Bride' always puts me in mind of cranberry sauce, myself."

Lindsey side-eyed him. "For me it's Mendelssohn's 'Wedding March' and sweet potato casserole, but there's no accounting for taste."

Jason said, "As in why anyone eats that stuff?"

Ashlyn shrugged. "Someone must like it because it keeps getting made."

"They say that about green bean casserole too. If your plans fall through, Jason, I'll make arrangements for my mother to play the Hornpipe from Handel's Water Music to set your mood for turkey stuffing." Lindsey lifted her violin. "So, shall we repeat that last one? And everyone, what makes or breaks this arrangement is our dynamics, so most of all, listen to each other."

CHAPTER TWENTY-TWO

Enrique felt rather than saw Parker in the classroom doorway. Either this was Parker's lunch period or else he was cutting class to intercept him, but Enrique wasn't going to bother about which. "Come on in."

Enrique didn't get up from the desk, and in fact didn't even look up from the middle school performance program he was reviewing. He'd already flagged two misspellings and noticed one kid's name had been left off.

Parker didn't move. "I want to quit."

No, you don't. Looking up, Enrique kept his expression bland because handling this badly *would* make Parker quit —and in no way did Parker want to quit the chorus. If he wanted to quit, all he needed to do was not show up this afternoon.

What he wanted was a fight. That, at least, Enrique knew how to handle.

Enrique set down his pen. "Talk to me."

"I just talked to you. I want to quit." Parker folded his arms. "I told you not to hurt my sister, and what's the first thing you did?"

Enrique said, "How are your brothers doing?"

"Hannah says they're back with Mom, but of course I'm not over there to see them so how would I know?"

Enrique said, "When's your next class? If this is your free period, I'll drive you over to the grammar school so you can see Bentley."

Parker stared at him. "What?"

Enrique gestured to the parking lot. "I've got a car. There's a no contact order with your stepfather, but not with your siblings. I will drive you to the grammar school so you can be sure Bentley's all right."

Parker scowled, and in that moment, Enrique caught the briefest glimpse of Hannah.

It stung. As far as Enrique could tell, Hannah hadn't blocked him—but she also hadn't answered him. He'd texted twice, called once, and didn't leave a voicemail. More than that would cross the line into stalking, and Hannah already had enough problems in that department.

Parker glanced at the clock. Enrique said, "You're technically still in the community chorus, so if I claim we're going to the grammar school to sort sheet music, that looks like a community service hour. Which will be important if you leave the chorus, since you're going to need to start racking up hours again soon."

With his eyes narrow, Parker huffed. "Fine. Let's go."

Enrique left his stuff scattered on the desk, but he locked the classroom. There should be procedures for signing a kid out of the school, and he ignored them all. Parker could leave the school anyhow during his lunch period. It took four minutes to drive over to the grammar school, where Enrique signed them in. He said to Parker, "Do you know which classroom is Bentley's?"

"Aren't you coming with me? To make sure I'm not a violent maniac?" Parker side-eyed him. "Or are you too much of a coward to see the damage you did to a defenseless kid?"

Enrique gestured to the hallway. "Lead on."

At the kindergarten classrooms, Parker looked first in one door, then the other. Enrique had worked with both classes at some point, but never in their own rooms—and not before he'd dated Hannah. He hadn't even registered back then that Bentley was her brother. Parker finally said, "Maybe he's not here?" so Enrique picked a door and knocked. *I'm looking for Bentley? Across the hall? Thanks.*

With a hesitancy Enrique hadn't predicted, Parker knocked on the second door, and when the teacher opened, he said, "Can I see Bentley?"

A shriek erupted from inside the room—*"Parker!"*—and Enrique's breath caught.

Bentley crashed into Parker's legs with a squeal, and Parker dropped down to hug him.

The teacher glanced at Enrique. "Well. I guess Bentley knows who this is."

Enrique said, "If you don't mind, maybe keep this on the lowdown?"

The teacher nodded. "I'd heard there were issues in the home, but I haven't been instructed not to release him to anyone."

"It's fine. We're not leaving the hallway."

Enrique backed off. Parker knelt so he and Bentley were at eye level, and Bentley hugged him again, talking at speeds of two hundred words a minute with occasional gusts of two-fifty. He showed Parker his shirt, then hugged him again, then kept talking while Parker just listened.

How any of this was justified, Enrique couldn't understand. The mingling of families and police, the mingling of care and control—it was all a disaster for this family. Control your adult daughter by spying on her location and bank account and online conversations, but leave your littlest ones unattended on date night. Somehow the kids had bonded with one another despite it all. Parker resented Hannah for being dense about her mother's interference. He resented the little ones for being needy. But at the same time, loyalty drove him to step in and protect his sister.

Three minutes later, Enrique saw the moment that same loyalty drove Parker to feel protective of Bentley too. Parker asked something Enrique couldn't hear, and Bentley pointed at Enrique while answering. He nodded, then showed Parker a temporary tattoo on his forearm.

Parker brought Bentley over to Enrique. Enrique didn't get down at eye level. He just said, "How's Carter doing? Is he feeling better?"

Bentley nodded. "He's good. We went to a doctor with the babysitter, but he didn't get any medicine. We stayed at a sitter's house with two dogs, and there were other kids, and we did temporary tattoos, and I got this one because it's blue. We had cake both nights for dessert and then we went back home, but I didn't go to school on Monday so I missed Kelsey's birthday party."

Enrique shook his head. "I'm sorry. Did Kelsey have cupcakes?"

"Yeah, and everyone got a whistle."

Kelsey's parents must harbor deep hatred for the parents of all her classmates. "Did the teacher save you a whistle?"

Bentley nodded. "Yeah, but I gave it to Carter so he'd feel better. He didn't like the dogs at the sitter's house."

"That was nice of you. I'm glad Carter's feeling better."

Parker said, "I've got to get back to my own school now."

Bentley quivered. "Will I see you again?"

Enrique said, "I'm not sure when, but we'll figure out how."

Parker put a hand on Bentley's head. "Remember, don't tell Mom or Tyler that I was here. They'll make it so I can't come again."

Bentley said, "Can I see Hannah too?"

Parker said, "No promises. But she'll come if she can."

Parker said nothing on the whole drive back to the high school.

Although Enrique hadn't been conscious of worrying, seeing Bentley okay was a relief. They had no real connection (in fact, they had no connection at all since Hannah seemed to have dumped him) but calling the cops and staying alone with the two scared boys had left Enrique feeling urgent for their well-being. If he were honest with himself, he had to admit he'd thought about the boys during quiet moments and wondered whether they'd gone back home and whether the experience had left them scarred.

Back at the high school, Enrique said, "I'll write a note for your fifth period teacher, to excuse the lateness."

"Thanks." Parker folded his arms. "This doesn't make it right what you did."

Enrique pulled a notebook from his backpack. "Who's your next teacher?"

"Mr. Fenton. I hope Bentley doesn't tell Mom because she'll freak the freak out."

Enrique said, "Why did Bentley give Carter his whistle?"

"He said. To make him feel better."

"Right. Why is it Bentley's job to make Carter feel better?"

"Because he's not a total monster. It's everyone's job to do what you can." Parker folded his arms. "That's why it was such a jerk move for you to call the cops. You could have taken them home."

Enrique said, "It's good that you're all looking out for one another. The problem is when parenting your siblings prevents you from being a child. You need less supervision because you're fifteen, but you still need to enjoy being a kid. Bentley is five and needs to be parented, not to be a parent. Carter needs it desperately. Hannah needed her mother too."

Parker stared out the passenger window.

"I'm not asking you to forgive or even to understand." Enrique tore the letter out of the notebook and handed it over. "What I'm asking is for you to look at the big picture and see how all the different stories weave together."

Parker muttered, "Yeah, yeah. Like when we sing."

Enrique nodded. "There's dissonance in your family, and it's going to take work to restore harmony."

Parker got out of the car. "Whatever."

Enrique got out the other side. "Do you still want to quit?"

Walking away, Parker called back, "I can't quit. I need the stupid service hours," and Enrique finally relaxed.

CHAPTER TWENTY-THREE

The therapist invited Parker into her office, but Parker only pointed at Hannah. "Oh, right." With a smile, the therapist said, "Last week, Parker said he wouldn't talk unless you were in the room too because that would annoy your stepfather more than just him talking. I think it's an excellent idea."

Thursday afternoon. It was Hannah's new normal.

She'd planned to spend her waiting-room hour reviewing the music the quartet would be practicing later tonight, but Hannah still trailed them into the office. Anything to help her brother. Parker dropped himself on the couch and answered everything with single words (if the therapist was lucky) or grunts. A couple of times Hannah volunteered an answer, but the therapist gave her a friendly look it was impossible to interpret as anything other than, "I've got this."

No therapy seemed to be taking place, but their

presence checked a box for the judge. "Are you keeping up with your homework?" "Do you feel comfortable with the roommate agreement?" "How are you doing with the community service?"

Parker said, "I still hate Mr. A, but he brought me to see Bentley."

Hannah straightened. "He did?"

Although silent, the therapist was monitoring everything. Every move, every twitch of body language, every shift in tone.

Parker glowered at Hannah. "I went to his office yesterday to tell him he could go to blazes and I quit. He offered to take me to the grammar school, and I knew he was bribing me, but I went anyhow."

Hannah leaned forward. "How is Bentley? Was he scared?"

"He misses you." Parker stared at the carpet, arms folded, shoulders hunched. "He wants you to visit his class too. I told him not to tell Mom because she'll tell the school you're not allowed to come. He said Carter got better, and he wanted to show me his temporary tattoo and a new shirt he got in emergency foster care. He thinks the cops arranged them a sleepover with a babysitter that has a dog."

Hannah pushed back into the couch, biting her lip.

Parker stared off at the wall. "Bentley isn't angry."

The therapist said, "You thought Bentley would be angry?"

"He got put in a police car and hauled off where he couldn't see his parents. What else would he be?" Parker shrugged. "I don't even know if I can get back in to see him again, but Hannah should sneak in and see him too."

Of course, during school hours Hannah was in Brighthead rather than in Hartwell.

The courts didn't offer sibling visitation. Even grandparents didn't get visitation, so if this dragged on, Hannah had no hope of staying connected to the littles.

The therapist said, "Did it help to see Bentley?"

"It did, and it didn't? You know." Parker looked up. "So, Bentley said he missed another kid's birthday party on Monday, but on Tuesday the teacher gave him the prize all the other kids got. Bentley gave it to Carter to make him feel better. Which is nice, right? Except Mr. A asked why it was on Bentley to make Carter feel better."

Hannah looked up. "Are you kidding?"

The therapist said, "Why is it Bentley's responsibility to take care of Carter?"

"That's what Mr. A said. I didn't see it that way. Bentley was being nice, except after I thought about it, I realized Bentley had said it like he was the one taking care of Carter."

Cold inside, Hannah said, "He's just a little kid. He sees everyone else taking care of Carter, so he's doing it too."

The therapist said to Parker, "Where's the dividing line?"

"You're the therapist. I figured you'd tell me." When she didn't reply, Parker continued, "Bentley does look out for Carter, but I never thought about it like Bentley was being his parent. Hannah used to take care of me, right? When Hannah was off at college and Mom had Bentley, I took care of Bentley. That's what family does. When Carter got sick and Enrique called the cops, I thought, what if Bentley thought he and Carter got taken away because Bentley wasn't good enough to help Carter?"

The therapist frowned. "That sounds like a dilemma."

Hannah wrung her hands together. "But you said Bentley was doing okay."

"Yeah, he thought his sleepover was totally fun." Parker swallowed. "Look, I don't want to go back home. Tyler is horrible, and Hannah's scared of him. He did something lousy and then did something worse. I went off on his car, and that was stupid. If I destroyed something, it should have been his face."

Awesome. Follow up a sincere regret with a worse threat. They were never going to be done with the Department of Children's Services.

Parker glowered. "Mom met Tyler right after Hannah

went to college and moved him in like a week later. Why the rush?"

Hannah said, "She was in love."

The therapist waved her down. "Parker's got this, and I want to hear his thoughts."

Parker folded his arms and tucked his hands under his armpits. "Last night I thought, it wasn't about us. It's about Mom. My dad walked out, but Mom had two kids with Tyler to lock him in. It wasn't because she wanted kids. She wanted to chain Tyler to her for eighteen years."

None of what Parker was saying was fair. Mom couldn't even defend herself, and here was Parker accusing her of everything under the sun.

The therapist said, "You sound angry."

He glared at her. "What was your first clue? Mom doesn't even love Tyler. Mom loves Hannah. Problem? Talk to Hannah. Something awesome happens? Tell Hannah. Need someone to raise your kids? Hannah."

Hannah bristled. "That's not true!"

"She didn't even notice me until you went to college." Parker glared at her with eyes as piercing as a nail gun. "You'd visit for the weekend, and if I got sick the Monday after, it was, 'I hope you didn't give that cold to Hannah.'"

The therapist said, "Are you jealous of Hannah?"

Parker looked stormy. "Not anymore. The price of being the favorite child is way too high. I'm not jealous of her. But Tyler is."

At work on Friday, Hannah kept startling at any unexpected sound, so much so that Dr. Griffin suggested she go for a walk.

Thinking of close-set trees and the bends in the road, Hannah shifted her weight. "I'd rather be working than not."

Dr. Griffin said, "I'm here if you need someone to talk to, but for now, maybe clean some equipment in the back."

There was always cleaning. Kennels to be disinfected. Floors to be mopped. Tables to be washed down. Equipment to go into and back out of the autoclave.

Glassware to wash. Lots of glassware.

Tyler was jealous of her.

Until Parker had put it together, Hannah hadn't ever considered what her mother's attachment to her meant to everyone else in the family. "Of all the children, I expect the best of you." "You're all I have." "I can't risk you leaving me." Hannah never considered how Parker heard that, or how Bentley interpreted it. Hannah had assumed because she was the girl, her mother felt closest to her. Nothing more.

Parker heard it differently: Hannah was Mom's favorite. Tyler must have heard it even more threateningly: Hannah was his competition. Mom thought Tyler was okay...to a point. When it came to love, Mom's love went to Hannah. When it came to meaning, to pair-bonding, to daydreams, to value—it was all Hannah.

No wonder Mom didn't want Hannah to marry. Mom had effectively married her.

"But that's not right." Hannah must have said it five times last night. Not right that she shouldered the entirety of her mother's focus. Not right that her mother looked to her for confidences and value and strength. Not right when her mother had a husband who should be doing all that.

"You're all I have" meant Mom didn't consider herself as having anything else, or at least anything else of value.

The therapist had said to Hannah, "What do you think about that?" and Hannah didn't know what to think.

"I think it's not fair of her to load all that on my shoulders." That's what Hannah was thinking now. "I think it's not right if she has to live her life through me. Or that if I make a decision, it's not just my decision because it affects her. I'm not her property that needs to be chained to her side for the rest of her life."

Except when it had come down to brass tacks, Mom had chosen to stay with Tyler rather than to defend her daughter and her son. Was it even true, then? Or was Mom doing the necessary work to hold onto Tyler on the grounds that over time, obligation and guilt would work their magic? Trained like a homing pigeon, Hannah would spread her wings and return to the coop. Mom had drilled those expectations into her.

Why shouldn't Hannah have a serious boyfriend? Why couldn't she hang out with her friends? Why shouldn't she move freely, talk freely, or even put her money in the bank freely?

Why shouldn't she grow up, move out, get married, and have a baby?

Mom had shot her full of guilt and obligation, but she'd disguised it as love.

She'd disguised it as unconditional support when in fact it was the opposite of unconditional. She'd called it protecting her daughter while she was gratifying herself.

Washing equipment was just the right task. Hannah had her back to the room, her face to the sink, and no one could see her tearing up.

Well. That was a trip. From being Mom's favorite to being someone Mom hadn't ever connected with at all.

Parker was disgusted whenever Hannah defended their mother. Enrique had felt the same—although her heart bled whenever she thought about Enrique, so she wouldn't. Susan had been outraged. The more they'd attacked, the more Hannah had reverted to the familiar position of being her mother's defender.

The excuses piled up in Hannah's head, but for once she quieted them. What if Mom didn't need someone to defend her? What if Hannah let Mom's actions speak for themselves?

Yes, Hannah's biological father had died early. Yes, Parker's dad had disappeared. Hannah had gone to college but had been required to drive home every weekend. According to Parker, there was a brief period when Parker was Mom's reliable one, Mom's favorite. Then Mom had met Tyler, and for a while Tyler took that role. After four years, Hannah graduated and came home. Suddenly it was back on Hannah again.

Parker thought Mom was evil. Enrique thought her mother was negligent. Susan thought her mother was neurotic.

What if Mom was a messed-up person with muddled priorities? What if Mom wasn't all good or all evil, only treading water to avoid the pain of losing her loved ones all over again? One at a time, she shored up everyone's loyalties in any way she could.

Not evil; human. Clumsy and unclear and damaged, but so very human. Humans made mistakes.

Hannah wasn't unfamiliar with mistakes. On Day One of Hannah's musical career, she'd brought home her cello to show it off to her mother. One of the strings was out of tune, so Hannah tried to figure out what their orchestra teacher had done to tune it. Even a half-size cello was massive, and Hannah had to lay it on her bed in order to turn the pegs.

It was a student instrument no one had played for years. The tuning peg was stuck, and Hannah couldn't get it to budge—until the peg cracked and the string snapped.

She'd stood there, stood over her beautiful cello that was now destroyed, fighting tears. A cello was expensive. The orchestra teacher had talked for a good fifteen minutes about how his littlest orchestra members had to take good care of their instruments—and she'd broken it on the first day.

Hannah tried to fix the string, but of course she couldn't. Stiff and oxidized, it had snapped right up by the scroll. There wasn't enough length to reattach it.

Terrified, she zipped the cello back in the case. She couldn't keep it there forever, though. She'd have to admit what she'd done. Her mother would be furious. There was no money, and they'd have to pay for this.

The next day, Mom picked Hannah up from school with the cello case in the back seat. "Hurry! I found you a cello instructor! He's going to give you three free lessons, and the first one is in ten minutes."

Hannah's lip quivered, but Mom didn't notice. Hannah protested that she didn't feel well, but Mom shushed her. "The orchestra teacher said you'll need lessons, and this school gives three lessons free, so you're going."

Hannah sat small in the waiting room while Mom played with baby Parker. Right on time, a tall man with salt and pepper hair entered. "Where's my newest cellist?"

Mom shook the teacher's hand, then turned to Hannah. "Sweetie, say hello to Mr. Castleton."

Hannah shrank into her jacket and tried to hide. Mr. Castleton hefted the cello with ease and led her into a practice room. "How long have you been playing?"

Hannah swallowed as he shut the door. "Two days?"

"Did you practice both days?"

She looked down.

Mr. Castleton smiled. "Your instrument wants to have fun with you. If you take it out every day and play a little, it gets more fun. That's why we call it playing. Why don't you show me your instrument?"

Hannah wrapped her hands around one another, and then the tears overspilled her eyes.

"Hey." Mr. Castleton pulled his chair closer. "Hannah, what's wrong?"

"I don't want to play. I'll just give it up." She swallowed hard, but the tears kept coming. She didn't want to give it up, but if he opened the case, he would see what she'd done.

Mr. Castleton said, "But don't you love your instrument?"

Her shoulders shuddered then, and she cried harder because she did. She did love it. The instrument had depended on her to take care of it, and she'd been entirely inadequate to the task.

Mr. Castleton said, "Then let's get you set up and see what you can do."

Hannah choked out, "I broke it."

Total silence in the practice room. He must be furious. He was a music teacher, so he knew how important it was to take care of an instrument. The longer he didn't speak, the more it hurt, and finally, Hannah looked up, terrified.

His brow was furrowed, but he didn't look angry. More like, concerned. "I'm pretty good at fixing instruments. Last week, there was a boy who left his violin on the floor, and he stepped right on it. Is that what you did?"

Hannah shook her head. She'd never be that careless.

Mr. Castleton said, "Have you told your parents or the music teacher?"

Again, she shook her head.

"If I can put it right, you know, you don't ever need to tell anyone."

They opened the case, and a frown contorted Hannah's face as she saw the big beautiful cello with its three perfect strings and one string waving free, supported only at the lower end. Then she opened the small zipper compartment and showed Mr. Castleton the cracked peg.

Mr. Castleton rubbed his palms together. "Well, let's get to work. Your first musical lesson is that instruments want to sing, and this cello is going to do everything in its power to heal up and sing again."

For half an hour, Bob Castleton took Hannah on a guided tour of the cello, teaching her the names of all the different parts, which ones were for form and which were for function. Nearly two decades later, she still remembered him saying, "Actually, they're all for function, even this beautiful wooden inlay around the edge of the instrument. It's called purfling, and it's there to prevent cracks in the wood from going all the way to the edge." While he worked, he replaced all four strings, one at a time. "This is the bridge, and if you loosen the strings all at once, the bridge collapses." He pulled out the broken peg, replaced it with a different peg, then tuned. Right at the end of the lesson, he examined Hannah's bow and showed her how to tighten and loosen it, as well as how to rosin it.

The instrument was perfect again. Hannah tried to dry her eyes so it wouldn't look like she'd been crying. Mr. Castleton was right: she could go back to orchestra and never say what she'd done.

"Now," Mr. Castleton said, handing her the bow, "I want you to play."

Hannah sat on the chair with the cello between her knees, and she made sounds. Her bow squeaked and the instrument grumbled, and Hannah flinched every time it squawked—but the whole time, Mr. Castleton seemed delighted.

He adjusted her hand. "Do it again."

Hannah shifted uneasily. "We're out of time."

"Just this."

She kept her hand in the better position and played again. This time the sound was stronger.

Thoughtful, Mr. Castleton nodded. "A cello has a lot going on. The strings need to vibrate. You need to press on the neck to change how long the strings think they are. The bow wants just the right amount of pressure. It's a lot to manage, but one day, you and the instrument will work together as if it's a part of your body, and when you're apart, you'll feel like something is missing."

Hannah looked up. "Thank you."

He stood. "Thank you for letting me fix your instrument. Let's get you back to your mom and set up the next lesson."

Mom wanted only the free lessons. Hannah ended up taking lessons for nine years. When Mom no longer wanted to pay for them, Hannah walked dogs for a neighbor and washed dishes for a new mom across the street. The cello became the most dependable constant in her life. It was how she made her friends and found her purpose. It was the only time she made sounds people wanted to hear.

When that string snapped, she'd been about to throw

away her love of music before she even discovered it. She'd tried to protect herself from pain, just like Mom was still doing. Hannah had damaged an instrument. Mom had damaged Hannah. You could damage through ignorance as easily as you could damage through malice.

Arguably a parent ought to know better. That was what Enrique kept saying. Either her mother didn't know or didn't care. Hannah would go with didn't know.

As for caring—Hannah still cared about Enrique. Even thinking about him hurt—hurt a lot more than cracking a tuning peg.

Chapter Twenty-Four

With the service chorus's performance list finalized, Enrique walked through the group handing out schedules and song lists. He said, "On the advice of someone who understands these things better than I do," omitting that it was Hannah, "we'll visit the same four places multiple times during the pre-Christmas season. It's better for the residents if they come to expect us on the weekends, and then our visits don't seem like a hit-and-run raid done for our benefit rather than theirs."

In his peripheral vision, Enrique saw Miranda's hand shoot up, so he said, "No, you're not required to attend every performance, but you should try to make as many as possible."

Parker was near enough to Miranda that Enrique got a good look at the kid as he scanned the schedule. One of the four facilities was a home for children with emotional and psychological problems. Some of those kids would be in residence for long-term treatment, and many were in state custody. The second Parker put that together, he'd likely detonate.

Miranda said, "You have us performing two places on Thanksgiving morning."

Enrique said, "Thanksgiving is a sad day for a lot of people. Many of the residential clients may not be able to see their families." Parker glared up at him, but Enrique kept his voice steady. "The facilities try to make the holiday as cheerful as possible, but even so, it's difficult."

Parker snarled, "Wouldn't it be better if whole families were together?"

Before Enrique could reply, one of the other girls said, "Not if you hear *my* mother talk about it!" and a couple of kids laughed.

Enrique said, "Anyone who's in one of these four facilities needs to be there. There have been social workers and doctors and, in some cases, lawyers making those decisions."

Parker rolled his eyes. "I bet it always started when somebody called the cops."

Miranda looked horrified. Word of Enrique's 9-1-1 call had gotten around, but Enrique would never break confidentiality. The answer was and always would be the same: he was a mandatory reporter. In the face of child neglect, he had no choice. A couple other teachers had approached him and confirmed calling was the right decision.

Instead of acknowledging Parker's barb, Enrique went to the piano. "Because we're visiting the same places multiple times, we'll need to increase the number of songs in our rotation, so let's get to work."

It didn't matter if Parker was angry. Parker was still coming to chorus, and if that was Enrique's only contact with Hannah, then that's what he had.

The fact that Hannah's parents would get nailed to the wall (or should have gotten nailed to the wall) was a bonus. The vindication still went through Enrique like heat, and part of him wished he'd witnessed the parental meltdown when they got home to find a house full of law enforcement officers. Let them make whatever groveling excuses they could. Enrique had unmasked them for the frauds they'd always been.

Hannah should have seen that instead of leaping right into the muck to defend them. Half the reason to call the cops had been for the external validation that her mother was a lousy excuse for a parent.

Well, no. The entire reason to call was for the kids. The kids were sick and scared and alone. Plus, Enrique was a mandatory reporter. That was the reason.

They got through the first few songs, Enrique keeping his eye on the clock so he could get in as many songs as possible before the school announced the late bus. "Time for one more," he said, and he launched them into "It Came Upon a Midnight Clear" while the seconds ticked down to dismissal.

These songs kept singing about peace on earth. They rhapsodized about goodwill. In stark contrast, Enrique's life felt like the opposite of peace and goodwill. All around was friction and suspicion. The Castleton family had no peace. With Bob drowning in the ever-rising waters of his illness, they had the opposite of peace. Hannah's life had no goodwill in it. Certainly none toward Enrique, and while she kept clinging to whatever peace she could make, it was the wrong kind of peace. Letting people use you wasn't peace. Capitulating so no one would fight wasn't peace either. It was just a different kind of ill will.

The song ended just as the announcement came. "All students taking the late bus, please report to the traffic circle." Enrique waved them off, and two-thirds of the students headed to the door, including Parker. After Parker left the room, the barometric pressure returned to normal.

Calling out wrongs wasn't disturbing the peace. Why then was Enrique un-peaceful? Every time he thought about it, every time he asked for affirmation and people reassured him, an awkward restlessness gnawed at his throat.

Maybe because the parents hadn't gotten nailed to the wall after all.

Maybe because returning the kids to the home made it look like no one cared about two little boys sitting out their parents' date night in a vomit-filled living room.

He stood over his desk sorting the music. He filed the attendance sheet marking off the students' volunteer hours. The whole time, his brain tracked the conversation of the few students who'd remained.

The state said Bentley and Carter were safe with their parents. For now. There would be a hearing and consequences, but Enrique had seen for himself that Bentley was doing all right. Enrique's duty had been toward the kids—and he'd done it.

That's where this all went sideways. He hadn't done anything wrong.

Could it be, though, he'd done the right thing for the wrong reasons?

If he hadn't wanted the parents punished, he'd still have had to call. He'd have made the call while sitting with the boys, and then he'd have broken the news to Hannah—and she might still have gone volcanic on him. If he'd only been thinking of the boys, though, he'd have been just as torn as she was. He'd have urged the social worker to keep in contact with him. Maybe the revenge Enrique thought Tyler would get on him was actually the revenge Enrique wanted to get on Tyler.

Enrique sat on the corner of his desk, rubbing his chin.

Miranda said, "Something wrong?"

Enrique said, "We keep singing about peace. What is peace?"

Miranda shrugged. "Everyone getting along and not fighting."

Enrique shook his head. "I've been in situations where everyone's doing whatever they have to in order to keep things from exploding, but there's no peace because they're all angry."

Miranda's friend said, "Yeah, that's not peace because sometimes people are seething and lying about how they really feel. Like remember how mad Aiden was about Lewis, so he kept coming and tell us about it over and over and *over* again?"

Miranda rolled her eyes. "Please. Every day he'd sit at our table at lunch and give us this detailed report of everything Lew did wrong. Can you believe he tied his shoe? In the hallway? Just because it had come untied?"

Enrique tilted his head. "Then what do you think peace really is?"

Miranda's friend said, "You should go talk to Mr. Craven because we had three whole classes on this in philosophy. But the definition I liked best was that peace works toward what's best for the other person at all times."

Enrique's brows contracted. "That can't be peace because sometimes in order to protect the other person, you'd have to fight."

She nodded. "But if *everyone* always wanted what was best for everyone else, you'd never have to do that. There's a time for standing up for what's right. But if you were, like, I don't know, trying to make sure some guy didn't divert a river and turn the land downstream into a dust bowl, peace would be wanting to make sure the upriver guy got his share of water too."

Miranda rolled her eyes. "And if someone's a bully, do we just go and make him happy?"

Her friend replied, "Bullying is the perfect example. If you don't fight back when a bully targets a victim, then the bully has peace and you have peace, but you've signed up the victims to receive violence. It's not peace for them. In order for peace to happen, the bully needs to be shut down—and that may require strong action. Depending on the situation, maybe even violence."

Enrique folded his arms. "All this Christmas peace we're talking about—you think it's not about putting down your guns as much as everyone firing together at the same targets."

Injustice. Pain. Isolation. Hunger. Despair.

By acting against Hannah's parents in anger, Enrique had deprived Hannah of an ally. He'd acted to save the children—which was absolutely the right decision—but his reasoning was the opposite of peace. He'd treated his 9-1-1 call like an act of war. It was no wonder she'd responded to it the same way.

The last of the students left Enrique's classroom, and he gathered his things to shut down as well.

The worst part of this was that Hannah had no reason to listen to him now. He couldn't honestly say he'd have done things differently. The act was right. The motivation was wrong. Without being able to name it, Hannah had picked up on his self-righteous attitude because all along, ever since childhood, that attitude had surrounded her.

He could have handled things differently and achieved the same outcome. Enrique had said he'd acted to save the boys. He'd only acted to inflate himself.

CHAPTER TWENTY-FIVE

First thing after she arrived at the vet clinic in the morning, Hannah called Cashman Lavera. "Guess who found your tracker?"

Cashman said, "Sounds great. I have your cat carrier."

"They're hardly of equal value."

"You'll notice I wasn't worried. When do you want to swap?" He paused. "Actually, before I return your carrier, I may need to bring you the cat. Remember how we knew he was sick because he kept looking at me? Well, for the last few days, he won't leave my wife alone."

Grinning, Hannah bit her lip.

Oblivious, Cashman went on. "He looks fine—and he's eating okay—but if she sits down anywhere in the house, he comes from wherever he is and gets on her lap. He's never done that before. Could that mean he's sick?"

Hannah braced herself. "Is your wife pregnant?"

Dead silence on the other end of the phone. Aha.

Cashman sounded irritated. "How does patient privacy work in the veterinary world? Because if you said that in a waiting room full of clients, everyone in Brighthead now knows, and we didn't plan on telling anyone for a while."

Yeah, she'd nailed that one. "I'm behind a closed door in Dr. Griffin's office, so your privacy is intact. Congratulations."

He relaxed a bit. "Thank you. Cats can tell that? Well, obviously they can. He knew two days before she did."

She fought a laugh. "I think they smell the pregnancy hormones, and some cats find that irresistible. You're not the first person to ask this question."

Cashman sounded amused. "You're telling me if Braddy hadn't gotten sick, then he'd have blown the game for us?"

"Depending on if people realized he didn't normally plant himself on your wife's lap."

"Well, then." Cashman sighed. "I didn't realize I needed to have the cat sign an NDA, but at least I don't have to pay you a couple hundred dollars to repair him. Feel free to collect your carrier whenever you want."

Dr. Griffin opened the door, looking urgent. Hannah said, "I'll pick it up later. Thanks!" and hung up.

Dr. Griffin said, "Prep for surgery. Canine with a stomach obstruction. Room three."

Hannah rushed into the exam room where a tearful dog owner was hugging a golden retriever. "Okay, boy," Hannah murmured. The folder was labeled Dinsdale. "Let's get you settled."

The dog's abdomen was distended, and he was drooling. Hannah and the owner lifted Dinsdale off the table onto his feet, and he padded after Hannah into the back. She gave him a shot of sedative so she could shave his abdomen and leg, then started an IV. It took ten minutes before they were in the suite, Dinsdale anesthetized, and the surgery begun.

This wasn't the first time Hannah had attended an emergency surgery after a dog had ingested a polyurethane foaming glue. This stuff was a perfect storm.

It smelled and tasted sweet, and once a dog had eaten it, the glue would react with the stomach acid to expand and fill all the available space. Without surgery, a dog would die.

Hannah worked in the background, handing over Dr. Griffin's equipment and monitoring Dinsdale's condition as well as the time. It was delicate work, but with hands as sure as any musician's, the veterinarian cut, peeled, pried, and eventually removed a rock-hard mass of glue in the exact shape of a dog's stomach.

"Poor Dinsy," Hannah whispered. The glue-boulder thunked onto the specimen tray, and they began the process of closing up. Hannah kept checking the dog's vital signs, but all was well.

Dogs usually recovered afterward. Thankfully the owner had known to come right in.

The closing-up process took longer than the opening-up. Hannah kept glancing at that perfect cast of a dog's stomach at full stretch. You shouldn't see that. A stomach should be an empty space, tucked inside and functioning unseen.

Working in a veterinary clinic, Hannah witnessed too many secrets that the animals' bodies were supposed to keep. The foaming polyurethane glue, though—that revealed a secret in a way even x-rays and MRIs failed to do. She'd seen hearts pumping on ultrasound screens, but never with this detail: the folds, the texture, the channels through which life continued to flow.

With surgery completed, Hannah brought Dinsdale to a kennel to recover, then rushed back to clean the surgical suite. Dr. Griffin was out front talking to the owner. Now they'd have to catch up on whatever appointments had been bumped but not rescheduled. Emergencies did that. Cashman wouldn't get his magic wand until the end of the day.

They worked through lunch because that was the least-harmful corner to cut. Still, the image of that glue stomach remained lodged in Hannah's mind the same way it had lodged in the dog, too large to expel from either end. One bite of sweetness, and that dog had swallowed death.

Hannah hated emergency surgeries. It took all day to get back her balance. After she did the occasional Sunday shift at the emergency clinic, driving home on the lightless roads, she'd find herself remembering her various patients and wondering if they'd survive.

She never could follow up with the emergency patients because they came from all over the coast. At least at the clinic she saw them again. She'd be in the room tomorrow when Dinsdale went home. The owner would hug him. She'd have tears in her eyes and would apologize even though she'd done nothing wrong. Dinsdale would be excited to see her and would relish being told he was a good boy. They'd be together again, and the owner would promise to protect him in the future.

Hannah's heart swelled. She knew how it ought to play out. For the lucky ones, it did.

At the end of the day, with the waiting room finally empty, Hannah was free to bring back the detector.

"Hey, let me see the magic wand." Dr. Griffin looked exhausted, but tech toys were tech toys. One of the receptionists had a GPS chip on her keys, so she hid them, and Dr. Griffin used the wand to find the chip. When it lit up green, she laughed. "That's wicked cool."

Hannah slumped on one of the chairs, exhausted. "It never activated for me. I feel safer knowing it actually works."

Dr. Griffin passed it to the receptionist. Of course, it was another fifteen minutes (and full dark) before Hannah could extricate herself from the office, but at least she remembered to grab the wand off the desk. If she got to Cashman's shop without the wand, that would be embarrassing.

"I promise I'm on my way this time," she texted.

He replied, "I can stay open an extra half hour. There's always work to do."

Still, she hated being more trouble than she already was.

She set the tracker on the passenger seat, but then just for old time's sake, she hit the button. The light went red. Red lights should be bad, except not this time. Red was good. Red was safety, and the low red glow accompanied her to the shop.

That dog. That poor dog, struggling in pain to dislodge something that had gone in so naturally. But also, that blessed dog because his owner had looked out for him.

It was a good world when you could keep others safe. Cashman had looked out for Braddy. Hannah was looking out for Parker. In her own way, Mom had been looking out for Hannah.

At the mill building, Hannah slowed to make the hairpin turn, and as she did so, the interior of the car switched to green.

She turned. Gasped. Couldn't breathe.

On the passenger seat, the detector wand had found a signal.

Hannah idled in the parking lot, unwilling to turn off the car even though the detector had settled back to red.

Cashman came outside holding the carrier, then stopped at her door. "What's wrong? You're about to pass out."

Her ears rang, and she couldn't feel her hands. "I— It went green. When I turned into the driveway, it lit up."

"Okay." Cashman's eyes darkened. "Let's get this thing found. Are you okay to drive?"

He climbed in the back seat and took the wand. "Go up Main and then turn around at the town center. I want to know which quarter of the car the signal's coming from, and then we'll tear it apart."

He held the magic wand at different corners of the passenger compartment, and by the time she got back, he'd decided the tracker was either in the engine or near the front passenger tire. He flipped on the shop's flood lights and crawled all over the place with the most powerful flashlight Hannah had ever seen, plus had her holding another. Three minutes later, lying on the ground to look into the wheel well, he said, "Got it. I'm not removing this until you decide: are you calling the cops?"

Hannah lowered her flashlight and closed her eyes.

That dog's stomach had been rock hard, the dog coughing and drooling in an attempt to eject the obstruction. It would have killed him. It had gone down sweet and small, and it would have killed him.

The owner had cared enough to save him. She hadn't watched while the dog suffered, protesting, "There's nothing wrong. I never fed you anything rock hard and stomach-shaped. It's your own fault."

You don't blame the victim. When Hannah put it that way —in terms of an animal—it made so much more sense. You never blame the victim.

Cashman had looked out for Braddy. Enrique had tried to look out for Hannah. It was such a mixed-up world. For once—just for once—Hannah wanted someone on her side looking out for her. All her allies were already in place: Susan, Cashman, Lindsey...Enrique, if only she'd let him. Now she'd let the law do it. Firmly. Finally.

Tears filled her eyes, but Hannah's free hand clenched. "Yes. We're calling the cops."

Hannah shivered on the couch while Cashman phoned Brighthead's Finest, asking for the same officer they'd spoken to before. Brighthead was small; they would send her. Cashman microwaved a mug of hot water and made instant hot chocolate for Hannah, only it was thin and flavorless. It burned a line to her stomach the same way the foaming glue must have burned all the way down the dog.

Cashman called his wife to say he'd be late, and they treated conversation as a plaything. "Can you hold dinner for me? I'm saving the world again." He was disassembling a tablet at his work bench, the phone jacked between his shoulder and his ear. "Well, I mean, you could...but think how sad I'd be if I saved the world and then had no dinner."

Hannah and Enrique hadn't ever played that way. Over time, though, they might have begun bantering with a series of interlocking references that tied them one to another, to their separate pasts, to their mutual future.

Cashman's future had a baby in it, the thing she and Enrique had agreed was a permanent connection. A baby was the promise of everything. Everything you were, everything you could be, everything you could have been. You were signing it all over to the one you loved, and the little one you soon would love together.

Enrique would be a good father. Hannah...did not have a good mother. That realization was just as flavorless and scalding as the paper packet of microwaved hot chocolate.

"I'm not disputing it was my turn to cook." Cashman paused. "That's not fair. I don't save the world *every* time it's my turn to make dinner." Headlight beams swung across the ceiling, and Cashman set down his screwdriver. "The cops are here, so you'll have to finish impugning my motives later. Love you."

Love you. Such a casual way to drop a life-altering attachment into a conversation. Those two words were a negation of all the play-fighting that had come before, with the promise of a continuation after.

Hannah could have done that with Enrique, but the first I-love-you should be...well, serious. Shouldn't it? Was there a website where you could look that up? Google, *"How should I tell him I love him?"* But that wasn't possible any longer. She wasn't sure her feelings of love had survived.

His for her, if they'd ever existed, were probably dust.

Now she'd have to Google something else. "How do I tell him I'm sorry?"

She'd been wrong, and the certitude weighed down her gut and itched behind her eyes. Enrique had called the cops because he'd found children in danger. She'd gotten angry for exactly the same reason, as if his reporting what her mother had done was worse than her mother doing it.

Here she was, about to do the same thing.

Look out for the ones you love. Maybe all along that had been why Hannah found the veterinary work so satisfying, and why the hard cases didn't destroy her faith in humanity. She'd assumed the hard cases—the abuse, the neglect—were the norm, whereas the loving protection was a bonus extra. What if she flipped the world on its head? What if instead of assuming you protected people because they loved you—what if she assumed people protected what they loved? What if she assumed people sacrificed for one another rather than expecting others to sacrifice for them?

No, Enrique would never love her now. She'd had everything backward the whole time. She'd loved him, and instead of letting him care for her, she'd sacrificed him right out of her life.

The officer arrived with the Brighthead Chief of Police. The police chief took notes while the officer got photos, and then in their presence, Cashman removed the tracker from Hannah's wheel well.

The police chief hummed. "That device is relatively clean. It can't have been on there more than a couple of days."

Hannah said, "He must have tagged my car when I was at quartet practice. He'd have known I park in the music school lot for a couple of hours."

"That's helpful. A music school may have security cameras." The police chief sealed the tracker in a plastic evidence bag. Good. Let Tyler lose his lunch when the tracker reported itself sitting in the police station. "I'll be in contact with Hartwell."

Cashman said, "If Hartwell PD talks to him, will they lead him out in handcuffs? Because if not, he'll have learned there's no ramifications to getting caught."

The chief nodded. "Handcuffs will be involved. I'm also going to get a warrant to seize his computer and phone."

Mom would flip. There would be tears. The little ones would be scarred, and Mom would blame Hannah for that too.

Time to stick the landing. Time for her mother to do the same thing Hannah had just done and face reality.

Time for Hannah to tell Parker what was going on.

Time for Hannah to figure out how to apologize to Enrique.

CHAPTER TWENTY-SIX

It was the second community service singalong of Thanksgiving Day. On the third floor of the rehab hospital, the students whispered to one another about the antiseptic odor of a hallway kept artificially clean.

Parker was staring at the ground, his face dark. Not for the first time today, Enrique wondered what was going on with him and Hannah. Parker had begun singing well—singing loud, singing strong. He'd relaxed with the other kids, and if Enrique wasn't mistaken, Parker was flirting with Miranda. Giving the kid a larger circle had been part of Enrique's intentions, but at the same time it ached because Enrique's own circle had shrunk when he'd lost Hannah.

"Enrique!" someone called, and he turned to find Susan Castleton. He hugged her, and then Susan went over to Parker. "You guys look great. Parker, you're coming home with me after, right?"

Miranda said with awe, "*You* know Susan Castleton?" and Parker flushed.

Susan said to Enrique, "Did Hannah invite you to our open house tonight?"

No, Hannah had not invited him. Hannah had not even spoken to him.

On the other hand, Hannah must not have told Susan that she'd cut Enrique from her life. Maybe she hadn't quite decided yet.

Susan continued, "Come over any time after eight. Tonight is just heavy appetizers, but on Sunday we're hosting the full meal. Hannah should have invited you to that too, but with all the chaos in her life, I should just have invited you myself." As though Susan's own life weren't balanced on the edge of disaster. "Parker volunteered to help me tonight since the quartet's performing and it's going to be...involved."

Parker added, "Mr. Castleton is coming for a visit."

Susan glanced across the room. "Yes, and thank you for the help."

Enrique followed Susan's gaze to where Bob sat in a wheelchair, his face blank.

This was awful. It was awful seeing Bob this way and had to be twice as awful for Susan watching the mind and heart she loved turn insubstantial as fog.

Enrique should go talk to him, but— But—

They had five minutes until the start. Grow up and deal with the discomfort. "I'll just go say hi to Bob."

Bob was skinner than he used to be, his skin loose on his face, his eyes duller. His quick smile was gone, replaced with a flat affect as he watched other residents get wheeled in.

"Hey, Bob," Enrique said. "I don't know if you remember me, but I was one of your students."

You could say that to any teacher after a fifteen-year gap. Bob hadn't been just any teacher to him, and Enrique hadn't been just any student. They'd lived intertwined for nearly two decades, and here Enrique was creating the polite fiction that under ordinary circumstances, Bob might not remember him.

With no recognition in his eyes, Bob said, "Yes, of course. Good to see you."

Heartbroken, Enrique sat on the nearest chair. "I have students of my own now. You were the best teacher I ever had, and I'm trying to teach them as well as you taught me."

Bob smiled. "Students are always something, aren't they?"

"They are. If you see that young man, next to Susan?" Enrique gestured, momentarily afraid Bob wouldn't remember who Susan was. "He's my new tenor. His sister plays cello, so there's music in the family."

Bob murmured, "Music should come from the family."

Enrique had no idea how to follow up. It didn't seem as if Bob felt tortured not to know who he was talking to, so at least that wasn't so bad. Enrique finally said, "We'll be coming back a few times before Christmas. I hope you like their performance."

Bob was focused on Susan, possibly the only face he recognized in the room. He murmured, "There's always song. She sings for me."

Enrique stood. "She does. And she's amazing. Happy Thanksgiving."

Susan was amazing. The more Enrique learned about her, the more amazed he was. Amazed by her tenacity. Amazed to learn she'd given up a baby and then waited years for Bob to come home for her. Amazed by how she'd raised her kids and kept welcoming new ones into the fold. Amazed by how faithful she was to her husband as he declined.

Amazed by how she'd reached out to Hannah. At a time when no one would have blamed her for remaining in place, Susan had extended herself yet again.

Similarly, Hannah had stepped into the gap to help Parker. She'd wanted to help her little brothers. No one was helping Hannah.

No, not quite true. Enrique wasn't helping Hannah because Hannah wouldn't let him. Susan was helping Hannah, though. The Department of Children's Services had been helping Hannah. Parker was helping Hannah.

Enrique brought his students to attention, then gave their starting note.

Even at a mere eight singers with only a handful of rehearsals under their collective belts, the kids did well. They knew the songs and projected their voices, and the few times he'd divided them into different sections, they managed to sing on key. Mostly on key. They opened their mouths. They smiled.

After each song, Enrique would step aside and look to the audience as they clapped. Most were older women, and some appeared very nearly comatose, but Enrique would seek out Bob. Bob, every time, seemed transported. The music triggered some part of his brain that longed to keep singing. Beside him, Susan had her hand on his, and Enrique wondered how she heard the melody as it echoed through Bob's heart.

Each time, he'd turn back to the chorus thinking they were good kids. As volunteer work, this was close to the bone.

After half an hour, the kids took their final bow, and Enrique thanked everyone for listening. (You couldn't thank them all for coming—not as if they had a choice.) Then he gathered the kids to him. "Great job! Go into the group now and talk to the residents. Tell them you're from the high school and we'll be back again a couple times before Christmas, and how great it was to visit. I'll see you all on Monday."

He had the kids break off, and Parker started heading over to Susan. Then, about three steps away, Parker turned back and stood in front of Enrique, arms folded, face grim

Enrique stiffened. "Everything okay?"

Parker stared at the floor. "My stepfather got arrested. For real, this time. Stalking charges. He was tracking her car. The music school had surveillance video showing him in the parking lot sticking a tracker into her tire."

Enrique's shoulders squared. "He did what?"

Parker glared away from Enrique. "There's been a bunch going on this week, and I told her to tell you. She's been saying yes and doing no, so I figured I'd just go ahead and tell you because she's going to keep chickening out forever."

Enrique's eyebrows shot up. "Is she okay?"

"Yeah, but Mom's acting unhinged. It's all a mess."

"Did they take the boys again?"

"They're still with her. I don't know if the judge didn't set bail or if Mom didn't pay it, but Tyler is cooling his jets in jail right now, and Hannah's all a mess."

Enrique shivered. "You could have told me."

"I could have, but she was like no, no, we bothered you enough. I'm like, you're still being bothered *by me* because I'm in the chorus. But the point is, tonight after they finish playing for some Thanksgiving party, Hannah's going to Susan's open house. Around ten o'clock or ten thirty. She's not staying long, but she's got to show up to get me."

Enrique nodded. "Ah. That's good information to know."

Parker glanced off to the side. "Well, you didn't hear it from me."

With a sly smile, Enrique pitched his voice very low. "Of course not. You were right here when Susan invited me to her open house. After all Susan's gone through, I'd hate to disappoint her."

Parker's mouth turned up into just the hint of a smile. "Dude. You're all right."

In music, in relationships, in everything…timing was key. Not just the time signature or the beats per minute, but also the timing of when you entered, when you crescendoed, the rate of crescendo...the time to walk in the front door.

The joke about basses was always, "Why was the bass standing out on the street? He couldn't find the key and didn't know when to come in." Well, Enrique was a tenor, but he still didn't know when to come in. Parker would have to text him when Hannah arrived.

Instead, Enrique spent his Thanksgiving waiting tables at the family restaurant. The place wouldn't be packed, but they'd have a few large parties, and it made sense to allow as many waitstaff as possible to stay home with their families. Ironically, by working, Enrique was spending the holiday with his.

Meanwhile, in a town twenty miles from here, Hannah would be playing cello at a Thanksgiving dinner in a hall packed with people barely listening. She would be surrounded by the quartet, which was becoming her family.

Parker would be pitching in at the Castleton home while Susan and Corwin visited with Bob, and then Corwin would be driving Bob back to the hospital while Parker and Susan cycled appetizers in and out of the oven.

Musicians tracked everything. They tracked the other players. They tracked the audience. They tracked the score in front of them. They mentally tracked the woman they loved in another town, only what was she thinking as she played? Was she herself tracking her mother with the two boys and a stepfather in a jail cell?

Enrique didn't sing tonight as he waited tables. He smiled and made small talk. He refilled drinks and brought an entree back to the kitchen when someone complained. He kept the chips and salsa coming and warned everyone to be careful because the plates were hot. He pocketed the tips without counting them, and then at the end of the evening, he paced behind the kitchen doors while a party of twelve lingered over a cleared-off table.

In the relative quiet, he checked his phone. Parker had texted. "She's here."

He replied, "I'm stuck for a while. Keep her there."

Sharon drew up alongside Enrique. "I'll finish off your table. Go to her."

Enrique smirked. "You just want the tip."

"Of course I only want the tip." Sharon kissed him on the cheek. "Go see Hannah. Find out if Thanksgiving is the right time to talk sense to her."

Talk sense, no. Apologize, yes. After you messed up this monumentally, it was always the right time for an apology.

Enrique parked halfway up the block from the Castleton home, the caboose behind the last of the cars lining the curb. Castleton events drew dozens, and Enrique walked up the street with his breath coming up in clouds.

He texted Parker. "I'm here."

Even at ten-thirty, the driveway was stacked three deep with cars. Enrique pitied whichever poor souls were parked in, but most likely the cars at the front were Susan's and Corwin's, and Corwin would just crash there for the night.

As Enrique got close, melody spilled onto the street. Lure that many musicians into a home with that many instruments and anything could happen. Usually, it did.

If anything could happen, maybe something wonderful could happen too. Enrique would have to try.

The sounds surging onto the lawn resolved into a jam-fest. That might be Lindsey on violin, but it might also be Jason. That bass guitar had a flair distinctly Corwin. Someone had an accordion, though, and Enrique couldn't imagine who was playing that. Oh, and a saxophone. And yes, detectable through it all was the strong bass line of the cello.

This hodgepodge of musicians was trading the main line of "Little Saint Nick" from one instrument to the next to the next. The main player would improvise while the other instruments backed up. How they could do that, Enrique had no idea, but he'd come to expect it of Bob's students. They knew how to make sounds that boosted one another without overpowering the main line. Then they'd trade cues as to which one would take over, and within a couple of measures all the roles would rearrange. Set it up this way and they could keep playing "Little Saint Nick" until well beyond the Feast of Saint Nicholas.

Three people were chatting at the end of the porch. "Hey, Enrique! Glad you could make it!"

"Table for twelve tried to stay forever," he answered, hand on the door knob. "I suspect they're squatting so they don't need a reservation for Christmas."

Inside the house, Enrique followed the music into the packed living room. The fire marshal would have shut the place down if he hadn't been over in the corner playing saxophone. Lindsey saw Enrique, and with something in between a physical signal and sheer telepathy, she passed the main line to the saxophone, who transitioned "Little Saint Nick" into "Little Deuce Coupe."

Howls of laughter, and a few of the guests began singing along. Enrique pushed his way through the guests and joined the song.

At the sound of his voice, Hannah jerked up from her instrument, her eyes wide. For a heartbeat, she stopped playing.

Lindsey met Enrique's gaze, and Enrique recognized the moment Lindsey made a decision. Really, you always wanted Lindsey to make a decision, even if sometimes you weren't sure what it would be. She might overextend herself—or she might just pull a miracle out of her violin case.

Lindsey took the main line back from the saxophonist, and while ornamenting it like crazy, took four measures to transition into "Let it Snow." The living room crowd sung right along, and Lindsey slowed it a bit. Then, after one verse, she changed to, "I Heard the Bells on Christmas Day."

That appeared to be a tactical error on Lindsey's part. Far fewer people knew the words, so most of them dropped out. Except Lindsey knew perfectly well that Enrique knew the words.

He'd play along. Well, sing along.

Peace on earth, good will to men.

Lindsey got right in front of Hannah so they could coordinate the main line between the violin and the cello. Then after one verse, Lindsey dropped out too.

Enrique stepped forward and soloed the lyrics. Lindsey backed to the wall, eyebrows arched, and accompanied very softly. The other instruments followed suit so the main line was all Hannah's, and she looked simultaneously helpless and perfectly in control. Under her fingers, her instrument crooned, and Enrique kept singing.

And in despair, I bowed my head. There is no peace on earth, I said.

No, there wasn't peace. Not when people were acting in anger. Not when they were looking at children as pawns to give them attention. Pawns to satisfy their anger.

Hannah played all around Enrique, filling the spaces and supporting his voice. She'd studied that video with Bob— she must have. After saying she didn't understand how Bob had done it, here she was doing the same thing...and doing it wondrously.

Then pealed the bells more loud and deep: God is not dead, nor does He sleep.

Enrique kept his voice firm and steady while Hannah's instrument surged forward then pulled back like the tide.

They weren't perfect. But for a jam session, this was spectacular. Fluid. Harmonic. The more they worked together, the more she relaxed, and then she was smiling. Lindsey joined back in. By now the saxophone was itching to take over, so Enrique wrapped it up.

Peace on earth, good will to men.

Peace. If Enrique could give Hannah nothing else, he had to give her peace. Either peace between them, or else peace for her alone by backing off. He'd ask forgiveness, and then he'd let her decide which peace she preferred.

The saxophone transitioned them into "Angels from the Realms of Glory," and Enrique backed to the wall just to watch Hannah play.

The song built to a crescendo, and then they all flourished to end it. Enrique applauded with the rest as Lindsey bowed, and then the saxophonist. Hannah bowed too, and she turned to put her cello away. Parker hurried across the room to her, and so did Lindsey. A moment after, Parker was putting her cello back in the case, and Hannah was in front of Enrique, shifting her weight, hands clasped.

She wrapped her arms around her waist, looking down. "I didn't realize you'd be here."

"Susan invited me." Too many people milled around, and Enrique put a hand on her arm to guide her toward the hallway. "Are you having a decent Thanksgiving?"

Although she nodded, she still wouldn't meet his eyes.

They stepped into the welcome chill on the front porch. Even with all the windows open, Susan's house was roasting with so many warm bodies moving around. On the porch, though, there were still three guests on the swing and one additional person standing against the railing. This was a Castleton event—of course it was littered with people. Enrique said, "Grab your coat and come with me."

She went down the porch steps. "It's not that cold."

Not cold compared to the house, but she'd get cold soon. He at least had his jacket. Rather than object, Enrique followed her.

Maybe she'd already reached some kind of peace inside. Two people couldn't make music together spontaneously without at least a small degree of trust.

If she trusted him, they could work this out.

Without meeting his eyes, Hannah said, "You were right. I had my stepfather arrested."

She turned toward the side of the house. Apparently they were going to hang out in the yard. Enrique said, "That stinks. I'd hoped things would settle down."

"Tyler couldn't let me win. He was jealous of me, and me running away—that wasn't enough of a victory for him. He needed to own me or else I was still a threat."

Enrique sighed. "He turned into a win-lose situation, and he lost."

"It didn't have to be that way. He had the chance to let everything go." Hannah looked up at the sky. "You were right. I'm sorry. You were right to call the police for my brothers. I said a lot of awful things, but you were looking out for them."

"Hey." Enrique wrapped his arms around her. "They're okay now, right?"

"I have no idea. Everything is in flux, but the social workers are all over it. They don't think it's unsalvageable." Hannah bit her lip. "I don't know about the rest."

Enrique said, "The rest?"

She didn't answer.

He put his cheek against hers. "Are you saying it's unsalvageable between us?"

He felt her nod against him.

He held her tighter. "Even if we can't patch things up, I owe you an apology. I called the cops for all the wrong reasons, and I couldn't see that. Calling was the right thing to do. I didn't do it for them, though. I did it from anger, and then I got defensive afterward. You called me out because you could see I had the wrong motives, and then I took it out on you as if you should be grateful that I'd done something from spite. I'm sorry. I understand if you don't want to talk to me again."

She put her arms around his waist, shivering. Enrique said, "Actually, hold that thought," and he slipped his jacket around her shoulders.

Hannah forced a smile. "You carefully saved all your body heat and gave it to me?"

Laughing, he hugged her. "Well, maybe I can have some of it back again."

She tucked her head against his shoulder, and then Enrique felt heat of his own. In a low voice, he said, "It's not unsalvageable. It's going to be all right."

She glanced up. "You keep saying that. You keep making

me think it really will be."

"Because it will. If you're willing, we'll work it out, and it will be all right." He hugged her again, and finally she looked into his eyes.

That, on her face, was trust. In a moment when she had nothing else to hold onto, still she was holding onto him.

Enrique said, "I promise," and finally he kissed her.

CHAPTER TWENTY-SEVEN

Hannah showed up at the Castleton house at ten o'clock on Sunday to start prepping the official Thanksgiving dinner. Lindsey was already in the kitchen with Sierra, arguing about how best to cook a turkey. Behind them at the sink, Corwin wasn't arguing but was simply prepping the turkey however he wanted.

Uncomfortable, Hannah asked for an assignment and received a loaf of bread to tear apart into a bowl. It kept her hands occupied but couldn't keep her mind off what would happen next: Enrique would show up for dinner, and she'd have to find a way to talk to him. He'd have to talk to her. They'd reached a truce, but what if his feelings had changed? What had he felt to begin with? It couldn't have improved.

She had no idea what she wanted to happen, let alone what was most likely to happen. She might still love him. He might never have loved her.

Lindsey started laughing. "Remember the year Dad went over the turkey skin with Corwin's propane torch because he'd read an article about heat-blasting the bird? And Mom kept peeling potatoes while he tied the thing up and carried it down to the yard—"

Sierra pivoted from the counter. "Wait, what?"

Hannah's eyes widened. "A propane torch?"

Corwin turned. Today's t-shirt proclaimed, *I'm the loose cannon. You'll probably like me best.* "That was savage! Mom said, 'Where's your father?' and I said, 'He took the turkey outside.' So she carefully set down the peeler and went to the porch, but she couldn't see him—"

Lindsey added, "—because he'd hung the turkey from a hook under the deck, and when she got downstairs, he had eye protection on and had just fired up the torch."

Sierra had her face in her hands. "Gosh, no! You never said!"

Corwin said, "You were doing marching band for the Thanksgiving football game."

Lindsey was laughing so hard she was gasping. "Mom walked back inside without a word and kept peeling potatoes. I went to shut the sliding glass door, and she said, 'Please leave it open so I know if I need to call the fire department. Or an ambulance.'"

Hannah laughed, then choked it back. She wouldn't have thought she'd ever laugh about family calling 9-1-1—and yet—

Corwin smirked. "Dad had to sneak back in with the turkey because the string had caught fire or something, and he didn't want her to see the damage."

Lindsey said, "Didn't the turkey actually fall off the hook?"

"We'll never know because he didn't say, and Mom played stupid. 'Oh, you brought the turkey outside? Why? Sun-drying it? Why are you holding one side against your chest?'"

Grinning, Hannah kept tearing up a loaf of bread into a giant metal bowl for the stuffing.

A family. She'd love to have a family like this, with people doing crazy things, other people accepting it, and everyone glued together by love.

Sierra said to Corwin, "What are you doing?"

Corwin didn't look at her. "Does it even matter? I'm not setting the bird on fire with an oxy acetylene torch."

Lindsey said, "Because that's all the options we have. Either you roast the bird until it's sawdust, or else you set it on fire with a torch."

Corwin raised his eyebrows at her. "I'm spatchcocking it."

Sierra exclaimed, "You're what?"

"It sounds filthy, doesn't it? That's why I had to do it. Don't tell Mom."

Lindsey looked over his shoulder. "He cut out the spine and flattened it. That's called butterflying."

"Overly sensitive Edwardian schoolmarms call it butterflying. I prefer the correct terminology." A crack sounded through the kitchen as Corwin snapped the ribcage and spread out the turkey. "Hannah, are you ever going to be done with the stuffing?"

Hannah cringed, but Lindsey said, "No," and Sierra said at the same time, "She's working on next year's stuffing, what do you think?"

Ashlyn trooped in through the front door. "We win! Thanksgiving food is on clearance! Cranberry sauce and rolls were all half off. Big bag of salad because I don't feel like chopping. Chestnuts, too. Does anyone know how to roast them?"

Lindsey said, "They explode. Give them to Corwin."

Corwin muttered, "Darn straight give them to Corwin."

Hannah brought the bowl of bread bits for Sierra to season.

Family. Someday, she wanted a family like this one.

She had a family, or at least she should. She missed Carter and Bentley, but she and Parker were a family for now. And someday, maybe someday she'd understand her own heart enough that she could marry and make a family of her own.

At noon, Susan Castleton returned from playing organ at the church services. "You guys! Everything smells amazing!"

Corwin bowed. "Entirely my doing."

Susan turned to Hannah. "Thank you so much for helping."

Hannah didn't have a chance to reply before Michael walked in with two grocery bags filled to bursting. They took those apart on the table, and in the midst of that, Enrique arrived with Parker.

Parker got one look at the kitchen and made a face. "Awesome. Because I didn't do enough cooking last Thursday?"

Susan waved him away. "You're off the hook. Go play with your phone."

Hannah got goosebumps as Enrique drew close behind her. "So Parker's *literally* off the hook?"

Susan paused. "I guess I did make that pun, didn't I?"

Enrique put his hands on Hannah's shoulders, and she relaxed back into him. "The community chorus sang at three places this morning. They did really well."

Susan turned. "There are officially too many people in this kitchen." She pointed to Lindsey and Sierra. "You two, stay. Everyone else, out of here. Actually, Corwin, set the table, and then you skedaddle too."

Ashlyn and Michael staked out the front porch, and Hannah transplanted with Enrique into the living room. Should she say something? How would they even begin talking?

Enrique solved that problem because he didn't seem to realize there might be a problem. Taking her hand, he guided her over to the couch. "There's a lot more space in here today. Last Thursday, I couldn't breathe."

"Before you got here, Corwin kept coming down from the music room with more and more instruments." Hannah rested her head on Enrique's shoulder, and the tension seeped from her body. "You could have played piano."

"With that many skilled players? I'll skip the humiliation." Enrique nuzzled her temple. "Any word on the kids?"

"Bentley's messaging me again. He says you're fun and asked if he can see you again." Hannah worked her phone from her pocket to show him the texts, all free of punctuation. "I'm trying to negotiate through Caroline so I can visit them, but Mom says not unless she's supervising. I'm getting better at this, though, because I've learned that's a control tactic."

Enrique squeezed her. "I'm sorry. You shouldn't need to defend yourself against your own mother."

Hannah's phone buzzed with an incoming message, and she laughed when she realized it was a photo from Cashman, captioned with, "Well, this happened."

The tabby cat had draped itself over one of Cashman's legs, eyes half-closed, chin on his thigh, and one paw outstretched across his lap.

A second text came in. "He still hates me, though. He waited until I wanted a snack, so now I'll have to starve."

Enrique laughed. "That's the pair you matchmade?"

She clicked off the phone. "They belonged together. I could just tell."

With his arm around her shoulder, he pulled her closer. "Can you always tell?"

Eyes half-closed like a comfortable cat, Hannah relaxed into the rhythm of Enrique's breathing, the motion and laughter in the kitchen, the creaking of the floor upstairs. This was how a world sounded when it fit together. It harmonized. The different voices worked in and out of one another, some crescendoing as others were fading, some strong when others were soft.

She let him surround her. "I can't always tell. But when it works, it works."

The doorbell rang, and Susan called, "Just come in!"

A heartbeat later, Lindsey exclaimed, "You? Didn't you have plans?"

From Susan: "Hush. I invited him special."

"You wouldn't want me to disappoint your mother." That voice was Jason's.

Enrique murmured, "Well, there goes the mood," and Hannah snickered.

Jason had brought a hostess gift (a plant) as well as a box of pastry, which left the Castletons a bit flummoxed. "We're not usually that formal," Susan explained, but the pastry went into the fridge and the plant went onto the table.

Before Jason and Lindsey had a chance to start bickering, the doorbell rang again. Susan called, "Hannah...?"

Lindsey's eyes had gone wide. "You'd better get that."

Hannah went to the door, hesitant, then gasped. Flinging open the door, she shouted, "Bentley! Carter!"

She dropped to her knees, and the boys swamped her. Laughing, she kissed them both, then buried her face in Bentley's shoulder. "I've missed you so much. It's so good to see you!"

Standing with the boys was Caroline. "I thought you'd approve."

The boys' caseworker was right behind. "We weren't sure we'd be able to get them for today, but your mother relented."

Susan joined them in the foyer, drying her hands on a dish towel. "Thank you for making it happen." She turned. "Linz, go get Parker."

"I'll do it." Enrique flew up the steps."

Carter said, "See my new shirt?"

Bentley said, "I have new sneakers, too! We've been going to an after-school program, and Dad's not going to be home for a while, but Mom said we couldn't see you, and then today she said we could!"

Hannah just kept hugging them, eyes closed, heart full to the top.

Bentley straightened. "Parker!" and Parker thundered down the steps to them.

Hannah stayed on her knees, face in her hands.

Caroline said, "It took a lot of convincing, but you've got them until five."

Hands rested on Hannah's shoulders. She reached up, and it was Enrique. He got down beside her and hugged her too.

She whispered, "You promised me it would be all right. And now they're here."

Dinner was fun. It was loud. It was chaos and at the same time there seemed to be a confident order to the whole thing. There were Castletons and Castleton-adjacents. There was a certain sadness because Bob wasn't here. There was anticipation because Enrique was with Hannah...but not quite at her side because Bentley and Carter each claimed that honor.

Corwin carved up the turkey with a knife sharp enough to split the atom. When she saw it, Susan exclaimed, "What did you do to this poor bird?"

Lindsey said in a warning tone, "Corwin, there are kids at the table."

Hannah added, "Kids who may not quite remember exactly how you pronounced this technique, and will get me in trouble when they repeat it to my mother in three hours."

Corwin muttered, "Fine. I *butterflied* it. It cooks faster and more evenly because it's flat."

Hannah said, "Thank you."

Carter gasped. "We're eating butterflies?"

Eyes glimmering, Corwin snickered. "Yeah, that's much better than anything I'd have said."

Enrique said, "Gives new meaning to 'butterflies in your stomach.'"

Carter recoiled, and Hannah whispered to him, "He's joking. That's a turkey, not a gigantic butterfly."

Carter pouted at Enrique with stern eyes, and Hannah fought a laugh. Carter said, "That's not nice."

"Mr. A is nice!" Bentley turned to Hannah. "Do you like Mr. A? I like Mr. A. He plays the piano at school."

Hannah glanced at Enrique. "Does he, really?"

Enrique looked shocked. "Bentley! That was supposed to be a secret!"

Bentley's eyes widened. "It was?"

Across the table, Parker smirked. "No, Bentley. The real secret is that Mr. A has a sense of humor."

Puzzled, Bentley turned to Enrique, who raised his hand for a high-five. "Oh, okay," and Bentley high-fived him.

Hannah said to Enrique, "Clearly I need to attend a school concert to hear you playing."

Bentley grinned. "He plays and we sing. Unless that's a secret too."

Hannah said to Enrique, "None of your secrets are safe with Bentley around."

Enrique mimed a sad face. "It serves me right for doing all my top secret activities in a kindergarten classroom."

Afterward, Hannah went into the kitchen to clean up, but Susan chased her back into the living room. "You only have the boys until five o'clock. Enjoy them."

Enrique was showing Bentley how to "play" a piano, and Carter was making an earth-shattering racket with a tambourine. Hannah dug in the music supply box until she located a pair of egg shakers, which were better-sized for Carter's hands and a lot less loud. Carter jumped around with them, and weirdly, Parker took a ukulele off a wall rack and started strumming. Bentley banged random notes on the piano. It sounded like an orchestra tuning up, except not as harmonious.

Enrique got down on the carpet beside Hannah and he slipped his arm around her waist. It wasn't long until she was leaning back against him, head to his chest, his breath on her neck.

"I'm glad you got to see them again."

"Me too." With a rueful smile, she added, "Maybe not so glad about hearing them," and Enrique chuckled.

Enrique said, "I think family is supposed to be like that. Chaotic. But fun."

Her family was a mess. Her half-brother was a mess, and the little ones were walking headfirst into an even bigger mess. If Hannah ever wanted children, she'd have to figure out what it meant to be a mother. But she had other role models. She had Susan, and she had time. She had plenty of time.

Hannah relaxed into his arms. "I'd like to have a family."

Enrique breathed into her ear, "I'd like to have a family with you."

Warm inside, Hannah closed her eyes. Enrique's fingers wove through hers, and she closed her hand around his.

A family with her. Him and her.

He loved her. She still loved him.

"Not right away," Enrique added, sounding concerned that he'd scared her off.

She squeezed his fingers to reassure him that he hadn't. "Give me a year."

Enrique said, "A year. Mark your calendar."

Hannah said, "Let's have a house like this, full of music."

"And noise," Enrique added.

"Happy noise."

"Happy noise and desserts. Music and love."

"Especially love." Rallying her courage, she turned toward him. "I love you."

He bent his head toward hers, and they kissed. "I love you too. I love you, and I want to make music with you for a long time to come."

With a barrage of shaker sounds, Carter crashed onto Hannah's lap and hugged them. "Me too!" he shouted, and Hannah hugged him back. Then Bentley was in the mix, and Enrique had his arms around all three.

Bentley said, "You'll make music with us all?"

Hannah said, "In a year, but I hope he will!"

"Of course I will." Enrique kissed Hannah's cheek. "Families should have music, and making harmony is what the best families do."

THANK YOU!

Thank you so much for reading Hannah and Enrique's story!

If you're in a situation where you're enduring domestic violence or emotional abuse, please reach out for help. Start with thehotline.org. For difficult interpersonal situations that don't rise to the level of abuse, check out *The Dance of Anger* by Harriet Lerner. If you are in an abusive parenting situation, please read *Toxic Parents* and the book *The Emotional Incest Syndrome*.

Thank you so much to my early readers, as well as to Mallory Crowe for cover design and Michaela DeToma for editing.

By the way, do you love Cashman? I do. Cashman comes from another book, but he's so much larger than life that he refused to stay in his own series.

You might want to check out our favorite dangerous Russian with the gorgeous hair in *Mischief and a Marathon*. It's the third book of the Brighthead Running Club romances, but you can read it as a standalone if you prefer. (On the other hand, Cashman is in all five books, so...?)

Who's the idiot who proposed twice on the spur of the moment? What's with the "bonding based on mutual disdain"? I think you'll have fun with this one. I certainly did.

maddie evans

Mischief and a MARATHON

The Brighthead Running Club Romances - Book 3

SPIRIT OF THE VIOLINISTS

Batting third in (and cleanup) is the pair I've been asked about over and over, and I'm so excited for you guys to finally read it.

In the last year, Lindsey has had to abandon the life she planned because her father is dying, taking over his music students and taking over as first violinist for his string quartet. Meanwhile, Jaon's been fighting at every turn, whether it's criticizing her, playing over her, or even double-booking the quartet. He's an amazing male, but such a selfish man.

Jason returned to Maine from Hollywood only because Bob was dying and needed someone to take over his quartet, so it's galling that Lindsey is in that position. Well, he sort of also returned to Maine because of the social media detonation that destroyed his California career. He'll be heading back in three months, though, so he'd better start putting those pieces back together. It's just that it would be so much easier if Lindsey would get out of the way--and out of his thoughts.

As Jason's California life seeps into his Maine life, Lindsey sees just what abandoned to help her family. Jason draws strength from Lindsey's confidence, but it's never going to work. He's going to leave—and good riddance. At least, that's what they keep telling themselves.

The Castleton
String Quartet

SPIRIT OF THE
Violinists

maddie evans